DATING HER BOSS

BY

LIZ FIELDING

MILLS & BOON®

All the characters in this book have no existence outside the imagination of the author, and have no relation whatsoever to anyone bearing the same name or names. They are not even distantly inspired by any individual known or unknown to the author, and all the incidents are pure invention.

First published in Great Britain 1999
Harlequin Mills & Boon Limited,
Eton House, 18-24 Paradise Road, Richmond, Surrey TW9 1SR

© Liz Fielding 1999

ISBN 0 263 81692 3

Set in Times Roman 10½ on 12 pt.
02-9906-51529 C1

Printed and bound in Spain
by Litografia Rosés, S.A., Barcelona

'Your carriage awaits, my lady,' Max Fleming said, with a sketch at a bow. 'Cinderella shall go to the ball.'

'Oh, right,' Jilly said. 'And who are you supposed to be? Prince Charming?'

'Isn't that supposed to be Rich Blake's role?' he replied, offering her his arm.

She pulled a face. 'Richie? He wouldn't know how. But if you're not Prince Charming, who are you?'

He tutted. 'You don't recognise me without my wand?'

She laughed. 'You're my fairy godmother?'

'God*father*.'

She laughed again. 'You look more like the demon king.'

'Wrong story.'

She turned her head to look at him. 'Maybe.' But, with his silver-streaked hair, saturnine face, dark eyes, Max Fleming looked thoroughly dangerous. And, despite his big-time television career, Richie Blake looked like a callow boy alongside him.

From boardroom...to bride and groom!

Dear Reader

Welcome to the latest book in our **Marrying the Boss** mini-series.

Enchanted™ authors will be bringing you a variety of tantalising stories about love in the workplace!

Falling for the boss can mean trouble, so our gorgeous heroes and lively heroines all struggle to resist their feelings of attraction for each other. But somehow love always ends up top of the agenda. And it isn't just a nine-to-five affair... Mixing business with pleasure carries on after hours—and ends in marriage!

Happy reading!

The Editors

Look out next month for the next title in our
Marrying the Boss series:

BIG BAD DAD by Christie Ridgway

CHAPTER ONE

MAXIM FLEMING was irritable. Seriously irritable. And his sister, at the other end of the telephone line, was being left in no doubt of that fact.

'All I'm asking you to do is find me a temporary secretary, Amanda. I'm not being difficult...' he ignored the hoot of derision from the other end of the line '...I just want a girl who knows what she's doing.'

'Max—'

Her attempt to stall his complaint was brushed impatiently aside. 'Is that such a problem?'

'Max. Darling—'

He continued to ignore the slight warning beneath the honeyed tone of her voice. 'Someone who can type accurately, take a little shorthand—'

'Your idea of a little shorthand does not coincide with mine or any of the perfectly competent secretaries I have already sent you,' she broke in sharply. Then she gave a little sigh. 'Not many girls do shorthand seriously these days, Max...' At least not the kind of girls she had sent to her brother, but then she and Max had entirely different agendas—a fact she suspected he had discovered for himself. But she wasn't admitting a thing. 'Wouldn't it be easier to haul yourself into the twentieth century and use a dictaphone?'

'Is this an admission that the famous Garland Agency isn't able to provide a competent secretary?'

His tone was rich with irony. He *definitely* knew. But Amanda refused to rise to her tormenting brother's jibe.

'I didn't say that, Max. But you'll have to give me time. Your standards are so high—'

'I haven't got time and Garland Girls are supposed to be the best,' he reminded her crisply. 'I'm quite willing to pay top rates for a secretary who can type accurately and take dictation a fraction faster than the speed she can write in longhand. Surely that's not too much to ask from London's pre-eminent secretarial agency?'

'And your temper is so short,' she completed, ignoring his question. 'You've been through some of the best secretaries in London in the space of a fortnight.'

'Best!' He left unsaid the obvious comment that, if they were the best she could offer, he never wanted to be within shouting distance of the worst.

'I have had not one word of complaint, nothing in fact but the highest praise for my girls from anyone else.' Which was true, but then she hadn't been mixing work with matchmaking for her other clients.

Max Fleming made a distinctly disparaging noise. 'Your public relations does you credit, I'll give you that. You've got every executive in London panting for one of the fabulous Garland Girls. They're a status symbol, the "must have" in every chief executive's penthouse office. They look good, they sound good and they mesmerise the men they pretend to work for into thinking they're privileged to employ them. Well, I'm not impressed by glamour—give me substance every time. Someone with a bit of grit in her character.'

Good grief—she might have chosen the girls for their looks and charm rather than their skills, but they hadn't been *that* bad. 'Nonsense. Admit it, Max, *you're* the problem here. Why should my girls put up with your bad temper and your unreasonable working hours?'

'For the money, sweet sister? Or have you simply

been giving them the opportunity to have a crack at mending my broken heart?'

'You don't have a heart.'

'You know that and I know that, but if you can find a girl who can manage a decent rate of shorthand I might be prepared to make the ultimate sacrifice.' He paused. 'At least until Laura's mother has recovered sufficiently for her to come back to work. I don't care what she looks like and I certainly don't give a damn who she went to school with—'

'Max Fleming, you have got to be the most impossible, infuriating—'

'I know,' he said, cutting her off in full flow. 'My faults are legion. If I promise to try and reform will you send me someone competent? Just for a few days while I finish this report for the World Bank?'

'I should leave you to type it yourself with two fingers, then you wouldn't be so—'

'Or are you going to admit defeat?'

'It'll take more than you to bring me to that, big brother. I'll have someone with you tomorrow. But this is your last chance. If this one walks out on you, you're on your own.' Amanda Garland frowned as she hung up, then turned to her own secretary. 'What on earth am I going to do with him, Beth?'

'Stop playing matchmaker and offer the poor man a competent secretary?' she said with a grin. 'Although where you are going to find someone who can take shorthand at the speed of light by tomorrow could be harder than getting him back to the altar. We're booked solid.'

'Didn't we have a CV the other day from a girl in Newcastle? She had some incredible speed.'

'Mmm. Jilly Prescott. You said that she didn't have

the look to be a Garland Girl, Amanda,' she said doubtfully, glancing at the photograph as she passed over the girl's CV.

'My brother has had his quota of Garland Girls for this year. He's going to have to take what he can get.'

Beth looked unconvinced. 'She's awfully young. He'll chew her up and spit her out before lunchtime.'

'Maybe.' Amanda Garland was thoughtful. 'Maybe not. He thinks our girls are more concerned with image than effort—'

'That's because you will send him all the pretty ones—'

'Well, he won't be able to say that about Jilly Prescott.' She regarded the photograph of a very ordinary-looking young woman with a mop of thick dark hair that would stuff a mattress. 'He wants someone with grit in her character.' She glanced at Beth. 'Northern women are supposed to be gritty, aren't they?'

'If you think he'll come to heel like a puppy, Amanda, you don't know your brother as well as you think you do.'

'It's worth a try.' And her mouth softened into a smile at the thought of what a little grit might do, cast into the smoothly oiled wheels of her brother's life. She tossed the photograph back at her secretary. 'Check out her references. If they hold up, call her and tell her to be here first thing tomorrow morning.'

Jilly Prescott dialled her cousin's number. It rang three times before an answering machine cut in with, 'Hi, this is Gemma. I can't come to the phone right now, but if you leave your name and number I'll call you back.'

'Bother!' Jilly pushed back an untidy wedge of dark hair from her forehead.

'Problems, pet?' her mother enquired, hovering anxiously in the doorway, making sure Jilly didn't chatter. She hated anyone making long distance calls.

'No. I've got her answering machine, that's all,' she replied, waiting for the familiar beep. 'Gemma, this is Jilly. If you're there please pick up the phone, it's urgent.' She waited for a moment on the off chance that her cousin might just be at home—willing her to be at home. Why did Gemma have to be out *tonight* of all nights? She continued, 'I'm just calling to tell you I've got a job in London and I'm catching the early morning train into King's Cross. I'll call you when I get to London.' She hung up and turned to her mother. 'It'll be all right,' she said, with more confidence than she was feeling. 'She said I could stay any time.'

Her mother looked doubtful. 'I don't know, Jilly. What if she's away?'

'Of course she isn't away—it's January, where would she go in January? She's out shopping, I expect. She'll call back later and even if she doesn't I've got her office number. It'll be all right, *honestly*.' The Garland Agency was the best in London and it wanted *her*. It wanted her *tomorrow* and who knew when she would get another chance like this? 'I'd better get on with my packing.'

'I'll go and run an iron over your best blouse, then,' Mrs Prescott said. Jilly knew her mother didn't want her leaving home, certainly not to stay with Gemma, and keeping busy was her way of hiding it, which was why Jilly didn't point out that she was more than capable of ironing her own blouse. 'Heaven knows what you'll look like when you have to take care of yourself.'

'I'll manage.'

'Will you?'

'I've been ironing my own clothes since I was ten, Mum.'

'I didn't mean that.' She paused. 'Just promise me that if anything goes wrong, if Gemma can't put you up, you'll come straight home.'

'But—'

'There are always other jobs, Jilly,' she said, and waited. A promise given to her mother was not something to be undertaken lightly. If she promised to come home, she would have to do just that. But, after all, what could possibly go wrong?

'I promise, Mum.'

There was an awkward little silence. Then, 'I suppose you'll be looking up Richie Blake?'

'I expect so.' As if they didn't both know that it was the one reason she wanted to go to London.

'Yes, well, he's a big man now. He might not want to be reminded of home.'

'We were friends, Mum. Good friends.' She still remembered the moment she had first set eyes on him, a pathetic new boy, small for his age, with white-blond hair and glasses held together with sticky tape. A bunch of bigger lads had been giving him a hard time and, despite the fact that she was a year or so younger than him, she'd rounded on them, given them a piece of her mind, standing over him like a mother hen with its feathers all ruffled.

After that she'd been stuck with him. Maybe that was why she'd seen more in him than most. Something special.

She'd been the one who had persuaded the PTA to hire him as a DJ for the Christmas dance; she'd sent photos of him to the local papers so he'd get some free publicity; she'd got her brothers to make posters on their computer, made recordings of the crazy patter with which he linked his shows and bombarded the local radio station with them until they'd given him a spot on a youth programme for little more than pocket money.

And she'd loaned him the money for his fare to London when he'd had a phone call offering him a 'jock' spot on one of the capital's commercial stations.

'You're a great kid, Jilly,' he'd said, as she'd stood by the train, waiting for it to pull out of the station, wishing she were going with him. 'You're the only one who's ever believed in me. My best girl. I won't forget you, I promise.'

'You are extremely lucky to get a chance like this, Jilly.' Amanda Garland sounded doubtful.

She wasn't the only one having doubts, but Jilly's had nothing to do with her ability to do the job. That wasn't worrying her at all. What worried her was that Gemma hadn't been in touch. And although Jilly had called her cousin from the station when she'd arrived in London she'd still only got the answering machine despite the fact that it had been the time of day when a working girl, no matter how late she'd been out the night before, should have been hauling herself out of bed.

And now, as if that wasn't enough to be going on with, she was faced by a woman who, having brought her post-haste all the way from Newcastle, appeared to be having second thoughts about giving her the promised job. Clearly her beautifully ironed blouse—she'd changed at the station from the jeans and sweatshirt she'd travelled in—was not making the kind of impression her mother had imagined it would. But in this sharp, glossy world anything she was wearing would look shabby.

She had done her best to portray the image of a smart, efficient, well-groomed secretary—as well groomed as a mop of hair that hadn't really been cut since she was ten years old would allow. She'd screwed it into a French pleat and anchored the loose strands with combs, but she could feel it threatening to burst loose even as she sat there.

It had worked well enough back home—certainly impressed the solicitor she had been working for until he'd retired a few weeks earlier—but in the glamorous world of Knightsbridge she looked exactly what she was: an ordinary girl from an ordinary little town in the industrial north-east. It would take more than a neatly pressed cotton blouse and chain store suit to disguise the fact.

She might have done better to have worn a pair of jeans and a plain white T-shirt, her hair in a pigtail—that at least was a classic any girl could aspire to. Except the woman who faced her across a vast acreage of immaculately tidy desk, her jet hair glossy, small white hands the perfect setting for the king's ransom of diamonds she was wearing on her fingers, undoubtedly wore designer jeans—the ones with the label stitched on the outside so you'd know how expensive they were. Jilly's, on the other hand, came from the sort of shops where, if you wanted to preserve any kind of street cred, you cut out the labels before you wore them.

Nobody was fooled but it avoided catty put-downs such as, 'I only buy my knickers from *that* place' and you just *knew* the cat in question meant her *everyday* knickers—not the sort she'd wear on a really hot date. Or, even worse, the teeth-curlingly awful, 'Good grief, my *mother* shops there...'

And now Amanda Garland of the Garland Agency was looking down her long, straight nose in a way that suggested she couldn't quite believe that she had offered Jilly Prescott a job of any kind—no matter how brilliant she might be on paper.

Actually, now she was sitting in a thick-carpeted, soft-focus office opposite the kind of high-powered woman she associated with glossy American soaps, Jilly couldn't quite believe it either.

She'd checked out the quality dailies at her local public library and made a list of secretarial agencies offering temporary work in London, then sent off her CV in the hope that someone would be impressed enough by her qualifications to give her a chance. After all, her qualifications were pretty impressive.

Now she was here, though, she had a sinking feeling that she was way out of her league. Only her stubborn Geordie pride refused to admit to the possibility that she might be second best in anything, stopped her from walking out right now. That, and Richie. The thought of him, of what he had achieved with nothing to commend him but cheek, a hard push and a following wind was more than enough to stiffen her resolve. Anything he could do...

'*Extremely* lucky.' Amanda Garland was beginning to irritate her. Luck, Jilly thought, mentally squaring her shoulders, had nothing to do with it. It had been sheer hard work.

There was nothing like a Royal Society of Arts Grade Three Typewriting Certificate with 'Distinction' to make even the Amanda Garlands of this world sit up and take notice, although Jilly knew that it was the infinitely rarer certificate, the one that promised she could effortlessly take down a hundred and sixty words per minute in faultless shorthand and transcribe it with equal ease, that had got her this far.

Of course Ms Garland had insisted on testing her anyway, just in case those desirable pieces of paper might have been the product of a bit of smart work with a home computer. Actually her brothers could probably have done a pretty convincing job if she had needed them to, so she didn't blame the woman for that. She just wished she wouldn't keep saying how *lucky* she was.

'Well, I won't keep you. I've told Max that you'll start this morning. Have you got somewhere to stay, Jilly?' she asked, glancing at the suitcase Jilly had brought with her.

'I'm staying with my cousin until I can find somewhere of my own. Actually, I need to call her and let her know I've arrived—' She had been about to ask if she could use the telephone, but she was already being ushered towards the door and she let it go.

Amanda Garland paused in the doorway. 'I'd better warn you, Jilly, that Max is a very demanding employer and he doesn't suffer fools gladly.' *So?* The question must have been written all over her face because the woman went on, 'He's desperate and he needs someone with really good shorthand, or...' The doubt was there again.

'Or?' Jilly repeated.

The other woman's brows rose a fraction at her directness. 'Or frankly I wouldn't have considered you for the position.'

'Well, that is frank of you,' Jilly replied, tired of being looked down on. The woman could keep her job. There were hundreds of other agencies in London and it suddenly occurred to her that, if the Garland Agency was prepared to bring her all the way from Newcastle because of her shorthand speed, she might just be in a buyer's market. 'Are my clothes *that* bad?' she enquired, with that native pertness for which her part of England was famous. 'Or is it my accent that's the problem?'

At home everybody thought she talked 'posh', but Jilly knew better. Despite the fact that her mother had insisted on elocution lessons with an actress who had been 'resting' ever since the war—which war no one had ever dared enquire—she was well aware that her voice still betrayed its origins.

Ms Garland's eyes widened slightly and her lips twitched in what might have been amusement. 'You're very direct, Jilly.'

'I find it helps if you want people to know what you think. What *do* you think, Ms Garland?'

'I think... I think that perhaps you'll do, Jilly.' And finally the creases about her eyes and mouth defined a genuine smile. 'And don't worry about your accent— Max won't. He'll only notice how well you do your job. I'm afraid my brother can be a bit of a monster to work for and to be honest I'd be happier if you were older. I'm rather tossing you in at the deep end.'

Her *brother*? Jilly felt her cheeks heat up. Amanda Garland was trusting her to work for her brother? 'Oh,' she said. Then, 'I thought—' Then with a sudden grin, 'Don't worry, Ms Garland, I'm a pretty good swimmer. Gold medal. Life-saving certificate.' Her smile came easily. 'And as for my age, well, I'm getting older by the minute.'

Amanda Garland laughed. 'Just keep that sense of humour and take no nonsense from Max. If he shouts at you...well, just be, um, *direct*.'

'Don't worry, I will. And I find that when men get particularly difficult, imagining them naked helps a lot.' Amanda's laughter turned into a fit of coughing. 'How long is he likely to need me?' Jilly asked when Amanda had recovered sufficiently to answer.

'His personal assistant is away looking after her sick mother and frankly we have no idea how long that will be.' Her face became grave. 'Several weeks at least, I should think, but don't worry—if you can work for Max you can work for anyone and with your qualifications I won't have any trouble placing you.'

'Oh, right. Well, thank you.'

'Don't thank me yet. Just remember what I said about standing up for yourself. And take a taxi. I don't want you getting lost between here and Kensington.'

'I've got an A to Z—' she began.

'I said take a taxi, Jilly. I promised Max you'd get there today, not at the convenience of London Transport. I'll call him and let him know that you're on the way.'

'Yes, but—'

'Go!' As Jilly still hesitated she said, 'This is an emergency! Get a receipt and give it to Max—he'll pay.'

Jilly didn't stop to argue. No one had ever wanted her badly enough to pay for a taxi before—if this was working in London it was no wonder Gemma was having such a good time. She picked up her suitcase and, holding the agency card with Max Fleming's address on it, she retreated swiftly to the pavement to hail one of the famous black London taxis.

She'd seen it done on the films and on television a thousand times but could hardly believe she was doing it herself as, clutching her suitcase, she stepped out into the street, stuck her hand in the air and yelled 'Taxi!'

To her astonishment a cruising cab-driver executed a neat U-turn in the centre of the street, pulled up beside her and opened the door from the inside. It worked! She climbed aboard and sat back, grinning broadly. It had been a shaky start, but she was actually beginning to enjoy herself.

The taxi came to halt outside an elegant house tucked away behind a high wall in a discreet garden square in Kensington. 'Here we are, miss,' the driver said, opening the door for her. She paid him what he asked and then boldly added a tip. He grinned at her. 'Thanks. Do you want a receipt?' he asked.

'Oh, yes. Thanks for reminding me, I'm not used to this.' She took the slip of paper he handed her and turned to the black-painted gate set into the wall and pressed the bell.

'Yes?' A woman's voice enquired from a small speaker.

'Jilly Prescott,' she said firmly. 'I'm from the Garland Agency.'

'Thank goodness. Come in.'

A buzzer sounded and she pushed the gate open. She had no time to stare up at the elegant façade of Max Fleming's home, or take in more than the briefest impression of his elegantly paved garden, the stone urns planted with evergreens, a small bronze statue of a nymph tucked into a wall niche above a semi-circular pool.

The grey-haired woman who had answered the bell was standing in the open doorway beckoning impatiently. 'Come along, Miss Prescott, Max is waiting for you.' She led the way through a spacious hall, passed a curving staircase and paused at a wide panelled door. 'Go straight in,' she said.

Jilly found herself on the threshold of a small panelled office. Beyond it an inner door was open and she could hear the low growl of a masculine voice apparently speaking on the telephone since she could hear only one person.

She dropped her suitcase beside the desk, slipped off her gloves and jacket and glanced around her. On the desk were two telephones, an intercom, a partly used shorthand notebook and a pot full of sharpened pencils. Behind it on a custom-built workbench were a state-of-the-art PC and printer. She wondered what software package was installed and, retrieving her spectacles from her handbag, propped them on her nose and leaned forward to switch it on.

'Harriet!' The disembodied voice had apparently finished with his telephone call and Jilly abandoned the computer, retrieved the notebook from the desk, grabbed a handful of pencils and, swiftly tucking in a slither of hair that was hell-bent on escape from her French pleat, she pushed open the inner door. Max Fleming was standing at the window looking out over the wintry garden and he didn't look round. 'Hasn't that damned girl arrived yet?' he demanded.

Jilly's first impression of Max Fleming was that he was too thin; too thin for his height and too thin for the width of his shoulders. It was an impression that seemed to be confirmed by the way his suit jacket hung loosely about him as if he had lost a considerable amount of weight since it had been made for him. But his hair was dark like his sister's, and, like hers, wonderfully thick and beautifully cut, the darkness only emphasised by a streak of silver at his temple.

That was all she had time to notice before he banged on the floor irritably with a slender ebony cane upon which he had been leaning. Then he half turned and caught sight of her. For a moment he said nothing, simply stared as if he couldn't believe his own eyes.

'Who the devil are you?' he demanded.

It would have been so easy to be intimidated, Jilly thought. His sister had already warned her that he could be a monster and, looking into a pair of eyes that glittered at her darkly out of his thin face, she believed it. And as they swept over her she recognised the moment for what it was. If she showed the slightest hint of nervousness under the challenge in those hard eyes she might as well turn around and walk out right now because he would take advantage of that weakness and run her ragged. What was it his sister had said? If he shouted at her, be direct.

'I guess I'm your damned girl,' she said, as directly as she knew how, and stared right back at him. She might be the wrong side of her twenty-first birthday, just, but she had never been scared of playground bullies and she certainly wasn't going to crumple now. For a moment the room was shockingly silent. Then Jilly, having demonstrated that she wasn't to be intimidated, pushed her spectacles up her nose and offered a truce. 'I'm sorry if I've kept you waiting, but the traffic was terrible. I wanted to come by underground but Ms Garland said I should take a taxi.'

One arched brow rose a fraction. 'Did she say anything else?'

Plenty, but she wasn't about to repeat it. 'That you would pay the fare?' she offered.

'Did she, indeed?' She'd hoped for a laugh, or at least a softening of that hard mouth into something approaching a smile. She didn't get it. Nor, she discovered, could she reduce this austere man to a mental laughing stock with a picture of him naked. Imagining Max Fleming naked wouldn't work at all, she decided as her cheeks, and just about everything else, heated up under the continued intensity of his unsparing gaze. It was as if he were looking right through to her bones, assessing what she was made of, and for just a second or two her determination not to be outfaced wavered.

'Well, someone will have to because I can't afford to go gallivanting about in taxis,' she said, determinedly forcing herself back onto the offensive. And she crossed what seemed like an acre of exquisite oriental carpet to place a small slip of paper on his desk. 'That's the receipt. I'll leave you to sort it out between you.'

Max Fleming's first thought was that she couldn't possibly be one of Amanda's sought-after Garland Girls. She lacked any trace of the style and the exquisite grooming for which they were so justly famous. She wasn't even pretty. Her eyes were hidden behind the owlish glasses, but her nose was too big and so was her mouth. Wide, full and simply bursting to smile given the slightest encouragement. And as for her hair...milk-chocolate brown, it was beginning to slide untidily from the combs doing an inefficient job of anchoring up the strands which refused to comply with her regulation French pleat. Then there were her clothes...

She was dressed in a neat white blouse and a plain grey skirt of undistinguished origin that stopped demurely just above her knee—an ensemble that suggested a school uniform. Then he realised it didn't remind him of a school uniform, she was far too tidy for that; what she reminded him of was an old-fashioned secretary, right down to the heavy tortoiseshell spectacle frames...

And suddenly it all became clear.

His sister was having a little joke at his expense, a little pay-back for all the trouble he had caused her. Any minute now this girl would fling off the spectacles, pull out the combs battling to hold her hair in place and reveal herself for what she undoubtedly was: a sexy-secretary kissogram.

Clearly impatient with his thoughtful scrutiny, the girl finally said, 'Are you ready to begin, Mr Fleming?' He was certain that whatever he said would set the whole wretched performance in motion, and there had been a time when he would have enjoyed the joke... 'Your sister said you were desperate—'

Desperate. Desolate. Empty. All of those things.

'It would appear that my sister has been more than usually garrulous.' But even if she was, as always, right, he could have told her that this wasn't going to help. He was beginning to think that nothing would ever help.

He pushed that depressing thought firmly away and concentrated on the girl. Was she an actress, down on her luck? Unlikely. An actress would have taken more trouble to excise any hint of an accent; an actress would have looked just a little more the part. This girl had to be a student of some kind making a little money to see her through her studies.

'What's your name?' he asked.

'Jilly Prescott.'

Jilly. Hardly a name for a grown woman and yet she was clearly that. Beneath the cheap tailoring there was the kind of old-fashioned hourglass figure only emphasised by the kind of waist that invited a man to span it with his hands if he felt so inclined.

Max frowned as the thought took hold. Then he shrugged, irritated by this further waste of his time even while prepared to admit that he'd asked for it. He knew he was difficult to work for and doubtless Amanda was sick to death of him and his demands for perfection; she was almost certainly outside in the hall at this minute, along with all the girls he had sent packing in the last two weeks, waiting to burst in and have a good laugh at his expense.

It was only that thought that stopped him from sending the girl on her way. No show, no pay and anyone who did this on a regular basis must be desperate for the money. He would just have to take his punishment like a man and then, maybe, Amanda would relent and produce the secretary she had promised.

And maybe in future he would remember to be more patient.

Maybe.

'Very well, Jilly,' he said abruptly. He might have to put up with it, but he didn't have to like it. 'Let's get on with it. I haven't got all day.'

He was holding himself rigid, gripping the cane top with his left hand, dreading the performance to come, but, instead of pulling the combs from her hair to let it cascade over her shoulders in the way he had expected, Jilly settled herself on the chair in front of his desk, arranged a row of pencils before her, selected one and, with it poised above her notebook, she looked up.

'I'm ready, Mr Fleming,' she said. Then she pushed her spectacles up her nose again and finally allowed her mouth to lift into a cautious smile, the kind one might offer a tiger with an uncertain temper. 'Whenever you are.'

CHAPTER TWO

FOR a moment Max stood mesmerised by the smile. It did something to her mouth, something unexpectedly sexy so that for a moment he couldn't quite take in what was happening, that she was sitting in front of his desk with a notebook poised ready for dictation.

She was *genuine*?

Still not quite believing it, Max crossed to the door and checked the hall. It was empty. 'Harriet!'

His housekeeper appeared from the direction of the kitchen. 'Yes, Max?'

'Did Jilly Prescott arrive alone?'

'Yes. Were you expecting someone else? You didn't say—'

'And no one else has turned up in the last few minutes—my sister, for instance?'

'Amanda?' she asked. 'Why? Are you expecting her? Will she be staying for lunch?'

'No, but—' She was looking at him a little oddly and, realising that he wasn't making much sense, he shook his head. 'No, I'm not expecting anyone. Just bring in some coffee, will you?' He turned to Jilly. 'You would like some coffee, wouldn't you?'

'Yes, please.' She knew from experience that the chance of drinking it while it was hot was so small as to be incalculable, but her day had started long before dawn and even cold coffee would be welcome. She glanced at the ornate ormolu clock on the mantelpiece. It was just after eleven. She hoped her stomach wouldn't rumble before she could eat the one remaining chocolate bar in her bag.

Max, returning to his office, noticed her suitcase, her jacket flung over the back of a chair. *Genuine.* Maybe. They would see.

He returned to his desk, propped his cane against it and lowered himself into his chair before picking up a sheaf of notes.

Across his desk, up close, Jilly realised that he was younger than she had originally thought. The greying temples, the pared-down bony features, had at first glance suggested he was nearing forty, but now she could see that he was younger than that—quite how much younger it was difficult to tell. Had he been ill? Or had it been an accident that had whittled the weight from him and left him walking with a cane? She didn't have time to give the matter any thought before he began dictating.

Max began dictating slowly, but he realised after a few minutes that she was keeping up with him without any difficulty—actually appeared to be waiting for him. 'Will you read that back, Jilly?' he asked. He still wasn't convinced of her probity and if this *was* some silly game his sister was playing with him he would prefer to know sooner, rather than later.

She read back everything he had dictated without hesitation, then said, 'You can go faster if you like. I take a hundred and sixty words a minute.'

He stared at her for a moment. 'Really?'

Jilly heard the disbelief in his voice. Didn't he trust his own sister? 'Honest,' she said. And just to emphasise the point she slowly drew a cross over her heart.

Max swallowed, hard. In another woman that gesture would have been blatantly sexual, but he had already been so far off right about this girl that he didn't know what to think. 'Amazing,' he muttered, and he wasn't entirely certain whether it was her shorthand speed or the girl herself who had provoked the word. But there had to be a drawback. 'Can you type?' he asked, suddenly suspicious.

'There wouldn't be much point if I couldn't,' she replied simply. Her face was solemn but a pair of perplexed brown eyes were regarding him through those large spectacle frames. She was puzzled at his caution and why wouldn't she be? 'Would there?' she pressed.

'I suppose not,' he said, disconcerted to discover that he wanted to apologise for doubting her. He rejected the idea out of hand—she still had to prove herself. Instead he continued dictating a complicated report, quite steadily at first, then faster, and finally at a speed that should have left her begging for mercy, that if he was honest with himself he intended should have her begging for mercy. She kept pace without apparent effort, her small hand flying over her notepad without the slightest hesitation even when he relayed long strings of calculations or foreign names, and he found himself going ever faster in an effort to have her call a halt. She didn't.

'That's it for now,' he said irritably. Which was ridiculous. He'd asked for someone efficient and apparently that was exactly what he'd got. The fact that she had the impudence to poke a little fun at him was something he could live with. At least she didn't fidget with her hair; she seemed blissfully unaware that it was threatening to descend untidily about her ears. 'How long will it take you to type that?'

'That depends on the software installed on your computer.' He told her what it was. 'No problem, I've used that before.' She glanced at her watch. 'I should be done by three.'

Now she was just being ridiculous. 'I'd rather have it accurate than rushed,' he said.

Jilly didn't bother to argue. 'Five past three, then,' she said, taking off her spectacles and rising to her feet. She paused in the doorway and looked back at him. 'I'll use the extra five minutes to make a cup of tea. The coffee has gone cold.' Max stared at her. Garland Girls didn't make tea. But then Jilly Prescott clearly wasn't a Garland Girl. Not by a country mile. Where on earth had his sister found her? 'I'll make one for you too, if you like,' she offered when he didn't move.

'No,' he began. Then, 'No, thank you. That won't be necessary. And if you ask Harriet, my housekeeper, she'll make you whatever you want.' Then as the clock on the mantelpiece began to chime the hour he continued, 'In fact since it appears to be lunchtime she'll make you a sandwich or something, too. You started late so you won't mind working straight through, will you?'

'Not at all,' she said, and Max Fleming was disconcerted to discover that he was quite unable to tell whether she was simply being polite or whether she was being just the smallest bit ironic. 'I did wonder what I'd do for lunch,' she added. 'Working through certainly solves that problem.' Ironic. Definitely ironic.

She went through to her own office and Max followed her. 'Where are you from, Jilly?' Max asked, and immediately regretted his curiosity. He wasn't in the least bit interested in where she had come from. She was just a *temp* for heaven's sake. Here today, gone tomorrow— at least if the last two weeks were anything to judge by...

'Can't you tell?' Her eyes sparkled as she looked back at him. Now she had removed her spectacles he could see that they were like the rest of her, just a little too large for her face, but quite unabashed by his scowl they were brimming with laughter, bringing his train of thought crashing to a halt. Hadn't Amanda warned this girl that he was a bad-tempered ogre who had been going through temps faster than the average person went through a page-a-day calendar? 'Ms Garland gave me the impression that she could cut my accent with a knife,' she continued cheekily, 'and serve it up in wedges with clotted cream.'

'Amanda was exaggerating.' Jilly's accent was elusive, not something to be cut, but spooned like warm honey over toast... 'But somewhere north of Watford, I'd guess,' he continued rapidly, disconcerted at the direction his mind seemed to be taking.

That was very nearly a *joke*, Jilly thought. 'Then you'd guess right. Home is somewhere no one has ever heard of, but it's near enough to Newcastle as makes no difference. Which reminds me, would it be possible to use your telephone? I'll pay for the call.'

Pay? She was offering to *pay* for a phone call? He was beginning to doubt his hearing. For the past two weeks Amanda's Garland Girls, with their designer clothes and perfectly rounded vowels, had been treating his telephone as if it had been installed for their own personal convenience.

'I'm supposed to be staying with my cousin but she doesn't know I've arrived yet,' she continued confidingly. Then, 'At least, she might do—I did leave a message on her answering machine...' She gave a little shrug as if suddenly aware that she had been running on.

'But you'd like to be sure?'

'Well, the thing is, I rang from the station first thing

this morning. When I arrived. I mean, it was early. *Really* early. I thought she'd be there.'

'And she wasn't.'

'No.'

'Perhaps she was out.'

'At that time in the morning?'

Innocent or what? he thought. Well, it wasn't up to him to suggest what her cousin might have been up to. 'Jogging, perhaps,' he suggested drily.

'It's a possibility,' she agreed, but not with any conviction. 'Anyway, I thought it might be better to wait a while and call her at work. I would have called from a box, but Ms Garland said you were—'

'Desperate?' A delicate pink suffused her cheeks as he filled in the word that she was suddenly unwilling to repeat, a delightful blush that turned this rather bold young woman into something a whole lot more vulnerable. 'I was,' he found himself admitting. 'I am.' Then because, as the target of those large brown eyes, he felt more than a little vulnerable himself, he continued abruptly, 'But you'd better call your cousin before you start. I don't want your mind wandering while you're typing that report.' He turned to go, then paused. 'And you'd better ring your family, if you have one. Let them know you've arrived safely.' Good grief, he was beginning to sound like a mother hen. 'They might be worrying,' he added more sharply.

'Might?' Her eyes fanned into tiny creases at the corners as she finally laughed and a dimple momentarily appeared beneath her cheek. Appeared and then was gone so quickly that he had to restrain himself from reaching out to touch the spot to convince himself that he hadn't imagined it... 'My mother will be wearing a track in the carpet pacing up and down waiting to hear how the job worked out.' Hoping it hadn't.

'Then you'd better ring her straight away…before the damage to the carpet is irreparable.'

'Ah, well, you see, I can't do that—'

'Why not?' He knew he would regret asking the question, but their conversation seemed to be taking on a life of its own.

'I can't phone her until I've spoken to Gemma. I promised if anything went wrong, if she couldn't put me up, I'd go straight home.' She gave a little shrug, little more than a lift of her shoulders. 'It's my first time away from home, you see, and she worries.'

He did see. His own mother had worried about him. Still did, probably, but these days she knew better than to voice her concerns. 'Then let's hope that your cousin had simply slipped out for a few minutes. If she's away you're in big trouble—'

'Away? In January?' Jilly was incredulous.

Max followed her glance to the window, to the overcast greyness of a winter day in London. 'Unbelievable as it may seem, there are places where the sun is still shining.'

'Expensive places.'

'Not these days.' He could see that she considered his idea of expensive and hers were unlikely to coincide. 'There's always skiing—' The word was out before he could stop it. Max had known it was a mistake to get involved. It was always a mistake to get involved.

'Gemma's not the athletic type.'

'Not everyone goes for the exercise,' he snapped. Then, more gently, because it was hardly this girl's fault that she'd reminded him of things he longed to forget. 'Some people are more interested in après-ski.'

And Jilly's head was suddenly filled with a travel-brochure image of glamorous girls and beefy blond ski instructors sipping *glühwein* around a roaring log fire in some snowbound mountain chalet. That was much more like Gemma's idea of fun. 'But if she's away I'll have nowhere to stay,' she said. 'I'll have to go straight back home. I promised—'

'Not before you've typed up that report, I hope—'

It had been an unforgivable thing to say—Max regretted the words before they were out of his mouth—but instead of throwing the notepad at him and telling him to type the damned thing himself, which was what any self-respecting Garland Girl would do, Jilly Prescott tucked a wayward strand of hair behind her ear and said, 'No, no, of course not. I'll get right onto it.'

Max stared after her for a moment. Was she being sarcastic? The question was redundant, of course she wasn't... This wasn't one of Amanda's usual hard-boiled temps. The girl had just arrived in London, was on her own, vulnerable. And that made him even more irritable. He didn't need this. How dared Amanda send him a waif from somewhere no one had ever heard of?

He wasn't interested in her problems. He didn't want to know. And yet something propelled him after her, urging him to apologise.

But she was already sitting at the computer, her fingers moving swiftly over the keys, wasting no time in starting work. Not even to make her telephone call. He wanted to tell her to do that first, but her back was stiff with pride, as great a barrier to communication as a brick wall.

It wouldn't have stopped him once, but it seemed that he had lost the gift of kindness, along with everything else...

'Are you ready for your lunch now, Max?'

He turned to Harriet, waiting in the doorway, watching them both. 'I've been ready for ten minutes,' he replied coldly. Then, 'You'd better organise something for Jilly as well.' *Jilly!* How could anyone be formal with someone called Jilly? He should have stuck to Miss Prescott. 'And show her around, make sure she knows where everything is.'

Jilly heard the inner door close and leaned back in her chair, easing her shoulders. She'd slept on the train—she could sleep anywhere—it was tension knotting her muscles, making her feel suddenly weepy. She sniffed, found a handkerchief and blew her nose. Weepy! How ridiculous. She never wept.

It was just that yesterday everything had seemed so simple. Too simple. If only her mother hadn't made her *promise*. If only she hadn't been stupid enough to believe that nothing could go wrong!

She blinked, straightened, tucked her hankie out of sight and forced a smile to her lips as Harriet reappeared with a tray, jumping to her feet to open the inner door for her.

'Thank you, Miss Prescott.'

'Oh, please, call me Jilly.' Harriet nodded and reappeared a moment later. 'I'll show you where the cloakroom is, shall I? I expect you'd like to wash your hands before you have something to eat.'

'I'm sorry to be such a bother. I'd go out but Mr Fleming is in a hurry for this—'

'Max is always in a hurry,' she said. 'Always was. Some men never learn.' Then, collecting herself, 'It's not a bit of trouble, I promise. What would you like?'

'Oh, anything. What did Mr Fleming have?' she said, trying to be helpful, make as little work as possible.

'Smoked salmon. Will that suit you?'

Jilly blinked. Smoked salmon? She'd tried it once, on a cracker, at a retirement party for the solicitor she had worked for since college, and hadn't been able to quite make up her mind whether she liked it or not. She could scarcely credit that anyone would put it in sandwiches for lunch. 'Cheese and pickle will do just fine,' she said firmly.

Harriet's face creased into a warm smile. 'I'll see what I can do. The cloakroom's this way. Come through to the kitchen when you're ready—you'll be more comfortable in there.'

The walls of the cloakroom were lined with creamy marble, there was a thick carpet on the floor, an antique gilded mirror and a pile of matching towels beside a sunken basin. It was a far cry from the lino and cracked mirror of the cloakroom in the office where she had been temping before Christmas. The kind of office she'd be going straight back to unless she got hold of Gemma soon.

Afterwards, when she had dried her hands on one of the soft towels, pinned her hair back into its combs and freshened her lipstick, she went in search of the kitchen.

'Sit down, make yourself at home,' Harriet invited.

'I really should make a start on that report—'

'Just because Max never leaves his desk doesn't mean you have to follow his example. Besides, you can't eat and type at the same time…' she waved towards a long pine table in a breakfast annexe, inviting her to take a seat '…can you?' Harriet was tall, elegant, her steely grey hair expensively cut; she was a long way from

Jilly's idea of a housekeeper. But then Jilly had never met a housekeeper before.

'No, I suppose not. But I have to make a couple of phone calls. Mr Fleming said I could.'

'If they're personal, why don't you use my phone? That way you can be sure he won't disturb you.' A hint of laughter as she led the way to a door tucked away in the corner of the kitchen suggested that she knew just how disturbing Max Fleming could be. The office was tiny, not much bigger than a cupboard, but there was a desk, a chair, a telephone; everything else was tucked away on shelves that lined the walls and suggested the room might once have been a pantry. 'Help yourself.'

'Thank you... I'm sorry, I didn't get your name. Mrs—?'

'Jacobs.' She smiled as she filled in the missing piece. 'But, please, just call me Harriet. Everyone does.'

'Thank you, Harriet.' But when she got through to Gemma's office she was told that her cousin was on holiday and wouldn't be in the office until the end of the month. She sat and stared at the telephone for a moment. Richie was the only other person she knew in London. She hadn't intended calling him until she was settled, until she could ring him and casually say, 'Hi, I'm working in London, thought I'd give you a call...' But this was an emergency and, after all, she was his 'best girl'. She found the number in her address book and dialled it.

'Rich Productions.'

'Can I speak to Richie Blake, please?'

'Who?'

'Richie—' Then she remembered. He was Rich now. Rich Blake, television's newest and brightest star. 'Rich Blake,' she said. 'This is Jilly Prescott. A friend,' she added, then wished she hadn't. It made her sound like some girl he'd met once trying to make it into something more important.

'Mr Blake is in a meeting.' The girl's unhelpful response gave the impression that was exactly what she thought.

'Then would you give him a message?' Jilly persisted politely. 'Will you tell him that Jilly Prescott called?' She repeated her name carefully. 'Will you please tell him that I'm in London and that I need to speak to him urgently? Ask him to call me back at this number.' And she gave the girl Max Fleming's telephone number. There was no response. 'Have you got that?' she asked, rather more sharply than she had meant to.

'Sure. I'll tell him.' And Jilly had a mental image of the girl crumpling up the note and flinging it into the nearest bin. About to say that she really was an old friend, that he would want to know she was in town, she restrained herself. Richie—Rich—was a celebrity these days. Girls probably rang him all the time and Jilly was getting the distinct impression that the bored voice at the other end of the telephone had heard it all before.

Her mother was rather more pleased to hear from her. Too pleased. 'Jilly! Thank goodness you've phoned. I've just found out that Gemma's away.' It was uncanny the way she did that. Just found out things. Where she'd been, who she'd been with. There had never been any point in telling her mother even the tiniest little white lie. She always found out. 'Your auntie has just been round showing off a postcard Gemma sent her from Florida. She's gone there with her boyfriend.' Disapproval oozed down the telephone line. 'I just *knew* it was a mistake for you to go racing off like that. What are you going to do now?'

She was being given a *choice*? She wasn't being ordered back on the first train home like a child? No, her mother was cleverer than that. She would rely on the promise given that she would go straight home if anything went wrong—a promise she had given in the certainty that nothing could.

She was twenty years old, for heaven's sake, nearly twenty-one. Not a child. A twenty-year-old, moreover, who had taken on a job, had people—well, Max Fleming—relying on her. Her mother would understand that, surely? 'Mum, right now I have half a book of shorthand notes to type up. Until that's done I can't think about anything else,' she said. But she was thinking that it would be nice, just for once, to behave like her madcap cousin, forget promises and do what she wanted.

Gemma was irresponsible, she dyed her hair and lived in London and her mother had always said she would come to a bad end. Maybe she would, but right now Gemma was on holiday in Florida. With a boyfriend. Jilly didn't *have* a boyfriend. Not that she hadn't had offers, but there had only ever been Richie and just lately he seemed to have forgotten she existed…

'What a disappointment for you,' her mother said, all sympathy now she was sure Jilly would be home in hours. 'What's it like? The job, I mean.' Certain of Jilly's obedient response to the jerk of the apron strings, she clearly felt at liberty to allow her curiosity its head.

'The job?' Jilly, who wasn't feeling at all charitable towards her mother, her cousin or anyone else, laid it on with a trowel. 'The job is *wonderful*. Mr Fleming was so eager to have me start that Ms Garland sent me here in a taxi. The money is four times what I was earning before and the office cloakroom is *marble*,' she added. A marble cloakroom would really impress her mother.

'Really?' Her mother's offhand tone and the little sniff that went with it were a dead giveaway. She was impressed all right. 'And this Mr Fleming, what's he like?'

'Mr Fleming?' What was Max Fleming like? She remembered the moment when he had turned from the window and stared at her. No man had ever looked at her quite like that before, made her feel quite that...transparent. Not that she was going to tell her mother that. Instead, with a flash of inspiration, she went for her sympathy. 'He's been ill, I think. He walks with a stick.' That made him sound positively geriatric, she realised belatedly.

'Ah, the poor man—' Mrs Prescott was all concern.

Geriatric was good, Jilly realised. 'And he's obviously had a terrible time getting a temp that can take shorthand down here,' she said, throwing in a sop to her mother's northern prejudices.

'Well, he won't be able to complain about *your* work.' Her mother's smug satisfaction about that irritated her. What was the point of being the very best at your job if you had to live at home and work in some dreary solicitor's office for a pittance? She wanted a job like Amanda Garland's secretary; she wanted to dress in a suit that cost a mint of money, have her split ends trimmed by someone who knew the right way to hold the scissors... Heck, why stop at that? She wanted to be Amanda Garland, not her secretary. 'What does he do?' her mother asked, cutting in on this wild daydream. Her mother had no objection to chatting long distance on the telephone at someone else's expense.

'He's an economist; he's working with the World Bank to find money to finance water resources for those poor little children in Africa. You know, the ones you see on the television.' Tugging shamelessly on her mother's well-developed sense of sympathy, she sighed dramatically. 'I don't know how he's going to manage...' Then, 'I'll have to go now, Mum, I've a pile of work to do—'

But her mother wasn't finished. 'Have you spoken to Richie Blake, yet?' She kept her voice carefully neutral, but even so the distrust seeped around the edges.

'No, not yet.' The plain unvarnished truth.

But the day was not yet over.

'Well, I'd better let you go, Jilly. Ring me and let me know what train you'll be on.'

Her mother's complacent belief that she would give up the best job she had ever had and return home without making an effort to find somewhere to stay until Gemma returned was practically an incitement to rebellion.

Promptly at three o'clock she tapped on Max Fleming's office door, entered and placed the completed report on his desk.

He glanced at the report, then at the clock on the mantelpiece striking the hour, and then sat back in his big leather chair and regarded her with those penetrating grey eyes. 'Tell me, Jilly, did you wait until you heard the clock begin to chime or was it pure chance that brought you through the door on the stroke of three?'

He knew the answer to that as well as she did, but she refused to be intimidated. 'Pure chance,' she replied without hesitation.

'In a pig's eye.'

Jilly blinked. Her solicitor would never have dreamed of saying anything like that. But he was right, of course, she'd been finished in plenty of time. She'd used it to try Richie's office again. He'd gone out. 'Whatever you say, sir.'

He looked quickly down at the report, but not before she'd seen his mouth twitch in a rather promising way. 'Max. Call me Max. And sit down while I check this for mistakes.'

'You won't find any.'

'Then it won't take long, will it?'

She didn't reply, but flinched as he checked some figures against a computer printout and then crossed through the ones she had typed, replacing them with a new set. He glanced up and this time there was no doubt about the smile. 'I had second thoughts about those figures. Reprint it, will you? Six copies. And call a courier. I want it biked over to the ODA the minute it's printed.' He saw her blank look. 'The Overseas Development Agency,' he explained. 'There's an address book on your desk. Not that they'll do anything with it until it's too late.'

Unable to think of any suitable reply to that, she picked up the report and headed back to her office.

'Then bring your book in,' he added before she reached the door. 'If I clear my in-tray tonight you can start working on it first thing in the morning. I'll be out until midday—'

She stopped, turned to look at him, her heart in her boots. There was no point in putting it off any longer, she would have to tell him. 'I'm sorry, but I doubt if I'll be here in the morning, Mr Fleming.'

He glanced up from the pile of mail in front of him. 'Not here? Of course you'll be here. Didn't Amanda tell you that I needed you for at least two weeks, possibly longer?'

'Yes, she did. But you were right. My cousin is on holiday—she's in Florida, so I've got nowhere to stay.'

'But that's no reason to go rushing back to...' He

paused, clearly trying to remember where it was she had said she came from.

'North of Watford,' she reminded him.

'Somewhere no one has ever heard of,' he retaliated. Then, 'She won't be away for ever.'

She might as well be. 'Until the end of the month.'

'Exactly. Two weeks. You can stay in a hotel until then.'

Just like that? 'I'm sure you mean well, Mr Fleming—'

'Max,' he reminded her.

'Max,' she repeated awkwardly. She'd never called anyone she worked for by their first name before. 'I've been temping since November and in case you hadn't noticed we've just had Christmas. I had to pay for my train fare down here on my credit card—'

'In other words, don't be such an idiot?'

'I didn't say that—'

'You were thinking it, and you were right. But you're not going anywhere, Jilly Prescott. You're the first girl I've had in this office in the last two weeks who even comes close to Laura...' he saw her frown '...my secretary. She's away looking after her mother.'

'Yes, Ms Garland told me.'

He regarded her closely. 'There must be somewhere you can stay?'

Must there? 'Any number of park benches,' she offered. 'And there's Waterloo Bridge if I provide my own cardboard box—'

'Don't be ridiculous!' he said angrily. The very thought of her sleeping rough sent a shiver up his spine. But there had to be some solution. He'd call Amanda; having found the perfect secretary for him, she would surely do anything to help him to keep her, if only to keep him off her back. 'Sit down.'

'What about this report?'

He didn't answer, simply fixed her with his eyes and waited for her to obey him. She returned to the chair in front of his desk and sat down without another word. Only then did he reach for the telephone. 'Amanda? I need another favour.'

'Please tell me that you haven't given that poor girl such a hard time that she's left already? I did warn you—'

'That "poor girl" needs none of your sympathy. What she needs is a roof over her head for the next two weeks.'

'So?'

'Can you find her somewhere?'

'I run an employment agency, darling, not an accommodation bureau.' He waited. 'I don't understand why you need my help,' she added unhelpfully.

'Who else would I ask?'

'Darling, look around you. You've got enough room in that barn of a house for twenty secretaries. Put her in one of them. She'll be handy when you get some brilliant idea in the middle of night.'

'I can't do that—'

'Why not? Really, Max, if you're worried that she'll think you're lusting after her luscious young body tell her that you're gay.'

'Mandy!'

'No? Macho pride couldn't stand it? Well, in that case you'll just have to convince her that Harriet will make a perfectly adequate chaperon, won't you?' And with that she hung up.

CHAPTER THREE

MAX replaced the receiver and looked at the girl sitting opposite him. Amanda's solution to the problem was so obvious that he should have thought of it himself. He just wished she hadn't put ideas into his head. It reminded him of his mistaken belief that Jilly had been a kissogram, that she had the kind of figure that would have made a nineteen-forties pin-up envious.

Jilly was looking at him expectantly and he swallowed hard. 'My sister always sees thing so clearly,' he said. 'The answer is obvious. You must stay here.'

'Here!' The blood rushed to Jilly's cheeks. 'In your house?' she added, eyes wide. 'But that's—'

It hadn't occurred to Max to take his sister seriously, but his offer appeared to confirm everything Jilly's mother had ever warned her about London in general and men in particular and he rapidly revised his plan to install her in the guest suite. 'There's a self-contained flat above the garage block,' he said quickly. 'It's not fancy, but it's a lot better than a cardboard box under Waterloo Bridge.'

Jilly couldn't believe it. How dared his sister call him a monster? Max Fleming was an absolute darling and she wanted to leap out of her chair and fling her arms around him and tell him that he was her knight in shining armour. His expression, however, and the stiffness with which he held himself, suggested that he would not welcome that kind of response.

'Well?' he said as she hesitated, dithering awkwardly

in front of his desk. 'What are you waiting for? I want that report on the Minister's desk today.'

'I'll go and sort out that courier,' she said. Then, at the door, she looked back. 'Thank you, Max.'

He waved her away impatiently, head already bent over a column of figures.

The flat was small but, as promised, self-contained. There was a stone staircase leading up the side of the garage block to a door that opened into a tiny vestibule and then directly into the living room.

'This is lovely,' Jilly said when, at last, Max had cleared his in-tray and Harriet was able to take her across to show her around. Max Fleming was right, it wasn't fancy, but it was comfortable and it had to be worth ten times anything she could afford. 'Why is it empty?'

'It was the chauffeur's flat in the old days. Max's father refused to learn to drive. Amanda and Laura wanted Max to take someone on after his accident but he wouldn't, said he'd rather hire a car and driver when he needed one—not that he goes out much these days.' Jilly would have liked to ask Harriet why, but she wasn't given the chance as the woman went on, 'I've brought across some basic necessities for you—tea, milk, that sort of thing—and the telephone is connected. Max said to tell you that phoning home is one of the perks of the job.'

'Oh, that's kind.'

Harriet gave her a sideways look and said, 'I'm sure you'll earn it. He works day and night and he'll have you doing the same if you let him.' She handed her a keyring. 'Here's the door key. The other key opens the side gate. Settle in and then come across to the house. Dinner is at eight.' Dinner? The flash of panic must have been visible on her face, because Harriet smiled reassuringly. 'Don't worry. Max won't expect you to dress up, just don't wear jeans—the dining room chairs are antique and denim is murder on the fabric.'

'Actually—' Harriet waited. 'Do you think Mr Fleming would mind if I skipped dinner? I didn't get much sleep last night and I'm fit to drop.'

'And he kept you working until nearly seven.' Harriet was sympathetic. 'You'll have to be tough with him, Jilly.'

'He said I could start late in the morning to make up for it. He'll be out until lunchtime.'

'Make sure you do that. And don't worry about dinner, he always works through it so I doubt if he'll even notice you're missing. Can I bring you something to eat here? You won't feel like cooking.'

'I'll just make myself a cup of tea and a slice of toast and fall into bed, thanks all the same.'

'Well, come across in the morning and I'll cook you some breakfast—you'll be hungry by then.' She didn't wait for an answer, but said goodnight and left.

Jilly closed the door and leaned on it, looking around her, scarcely able to believe her luck. Then a huge yawn caught her by surprise. It was, she decided, quite possible that she wouldn't get as far as making toast. But she had to have a bath. And phone her mother. That would take careful handling. What was she going to say?

I'm such a great secretary that Max has given me the flat above his garage rather than lose me? She could just imagine her mother's reaction to that news. She'd struggled to bring up three young children on her own and her opinion of men was not good at the best of times.

It was utterly ridiculous, of course—a man like Max Fleming wouldn't look twice at a girl like her. But perhaps it would be a good idea if she continued to refer to him as Mr Fleming... The geriatric Mr Fleming. The thought provoked a giggle as she rang home.

'Jilly! What on earth is happening? I've been sitting here all afternoon waiting, worrying—'

Jilly brought the giggle under control and quickly said, 'Everything's fine, Mum. Mr Fleming has offered me the use of the chauffeur's flat until Gemma gets back. If you've got a pen there, I'll give you the telephone number.'

'Where's the chauffeur?' her mother demanded suspiciously.

'He hasn't got one. The place was empty. I'll give you the phone number now, if you're ready.'

'Oh. Right. Just a minute, I'll have to find something to write with.' Disappointment oozed down the line and Jilly suddenly realised that her mother must have thought it was her lucky day when she'd discovered Gemma was away. Well, she wasn't about to give her time to think of some other reason why she simply had to come straight home.

She read the number off the dial. Then, before her mother asked any awkward questions—like, What kind of office block has a chauffeur's flat?—she said, 'Look, I'll have to go, Mum. This is long distance.' And she didn't feel in the least bit wicked for using her mother's excuses for her own ends. 'I'll call you tomorrow evening. Don't worry, now. Bye.' She put the phone down quickly. That had been easier than she'd thought.

It rang again almost immediately, making her jump, and she smiled a little grimly. She'd congratulated herself a fraction too soon. She picked up the receiver somewhat gingerly.

'Jilly Prescott.'

'I was just checking that I'd got the number right,' her mother said.

Just checking up on *her*, more like. 'Good idea, Mum.'

'And what's the address?'

She told her and then quickly said goodbye and hung up before her mother thought of any more questions.

She glanced at the telephone, wondering if she should try Richie's office again. She checked her watch and realised that it was nearly seven-thirty. Far too late.

She unpacked, hanging her clothes neatly in the closet. The bed had been made, presumably by Harriet; it took a real effort of will to drag herself away from the temptation of the turned-back cover and white linen sheets and to go and run a bath.

The bathroom wasn't up to the marble magnificence of the cloakroom in the house, but the water was hot and there were expensive bath salts and a pile of fresh towels just like the ones in the cloakroom. Too much of this, she thought as she sank beneath the water, and she'd be spoilt rotten.

The bath revived her sufficiently to reconsider the toast. She put a couple of slices of bread in the toaster, switched on the kettle and wondered again about trying Richie's office. After all, show-business people kept odd hours—someone might still be in the office.

The number had just begun to ring when there was a tap at the door. Harriet had decided to bring her some supper after all. 'Come in, Harriet,' she called, without moving from the phone.

But it wasn't Harriet. It was Max Fleming.

Max opened the door and walked into the small sitting room of the flat as Jilly, her hair loose now about her shoulders, turned and for a moment she was perfectly still in the soft pinkish light from a tall lamp on the table beside her. Invitingly dishevelled, her wrap hung open to reveal a baggy T-shirt that clothed her curves effectively enough, but only served to draw attention to a pair of shapely legs, the kind of thighs that—

'Oh, Max. I thought—' Then she swallowed nervously as she realised that one wrong move was all that stood between her and exposure and with a gurgle of embarrassment she dropped the telephone, grabbed for her belt and tied it about her in a manner definitely designed to deter rather than tempt. Her reaction, all flustered innocence, was oddly disarming. Most of the women he knew, caught in a similar predicament, would have opted for the wrong move. But then he was the first to admit that Jilly Prescott was not like any woman he had ever met before.

'You really should lock the door, Jilly. Anyone could have walked in.'

'Anyone did,' she responded, the pink spots of colour rapidly fading as, decency restored, she recovered her poise. 'I thought you were Harriet. Didn't I say, "Come in, Harriet—"?' she enquired.

'Harriet is busy, but since you're apparently too tired to come across for dinner I thought I'd better bring you this.' He held out a piece of paper but made no move to close the distance between them. She made no move to take it.

'What is it?'

'You had a phone call. A message from someone called Blake.'

'Richie!' Delight lit up her face and eagerness carried her halfway towards him before she recalled the informality of her covering and thought better of it.

'He's your boyfriend?' he asked, surprised.

'You've heard of him?'

Her pleasure that he might have was obvious, but there was no point pretending, he'd only look a fool when he was found out. 'No, sorry. Should I have?'

'Richie… Rich Blake,' she said. Her shoulders hunched in an awkward little shrug at his lack of response. 'He's on the television. We were at school together,' she said.

'Really?' Then, as the penny dropped, 'Good God, you don't mean that idiot disc jockey—'

'He's not an idiot!' She leapt to his defence like a tigress, then, perhaps realising that she was being ridiculous, that he had moved well beyond the point where he needed her protection—protection of any kind—she stopped. 'I've been trying to get hold of him all day,' she said, bending to retrieve the handset from the floor where she had dropped it, her long thick hair swinging untidily over her face. 'I was just going to give it one more try before going to bed.'

'Then I've saved you the trouble.' He put the piece of paper down on a small sofa table, held it there with a finger. 'Mr Blake must have finally got one, or all, of your messages…' he tapped the paper '…because his secretary said to tell you that he's busy this week but that he'll be in touch as soon as he can.'

Shock leached the colour from her face, dulled the sparkle in her eyes. It was as if someone had switched off a light inside her, he thought. Then she remembered her manners. 'Thank you,' she said, very quietly. 'I'm sorry that you were bothered.'

Max could see that a message via a secretary was not what she had been anticipating. Perhaps she was remembering how many times she'd been asked to call people with messages like that? He could hear himself saying to Laura, 'Tell her I'll be in touch when I have a moment…' The polite put-off. It was the 'Don't call me, I'll call you,' message.

She might have been Rich Blake's girl back home, but if she'd come to London expecting to pick up the relationship where it had left off he was certain there would be tears before bedtime. Rich Blake was the big new name in radio and now he was moving into television, making money faster than he could spend it—just—and duvet-deep in the kind of women who spent their entire lives devoting themselves to looking beautiful. Ambitious women who wanted to get onto the small screen; being seen with Rich Blake was a great way to get their picture in the paper and making Rich Blake happy was a foot in the door to fame. Jilly Prescott, he rather suspected, wouldn't stand a chance in that kind of company.

Should he warn her? Would she believe him if he did? She wouldn't want to and she certainly wouldn't thank him for his trouble.

'It was no bother.' He withdrew his hand from the message and glanced around. 'Have you got everything you need?' he said, changing the subject.

'Yes, thank you. Harriet has been very kind.' Then, rubbing at her arms as if suddenly cold, 'You've both been very kind.'

He nodded, crossed to the thermostat, turned it up a little. 'If you need anything come across to the house.' Then he looked at her. Her hair hung forward across her face and she made no move to push it back, using it like a curtain to hide her feelings. She was on her own in a strange city and there was no one to put an arm about her, hold her and tell her that everything would be all right. Only him. But he knew it wouldn't be all right and he wanted to push back her hair, look her in the eyes and tell her to go home, now, before she was really hurt. But he didn't move. She wouldn't listen and he'd lose himself the best temp in London for his trouble and quite possibly get himself landed with an accusation of sexual harassment into the bargain. He shouldn't have come over to the flat. He wouldn't again. 'Keep the heating turned up—the temperature's gone down like a stone,' he said. 'It's freezing out there.'

'I will. Thank you.'

Her eyes strayed towards the message. She wanted him to go so that she could read it, fool herself into reading hidden meanings in the words, and he fervently wished that he had stayed in the warmth of his study instead of venturing across the courtyard.

The fact that the message had been delivered via a secretary had fooled him into believing it was from some family friend or acquaintance who had been asked to keep a friendly eye on her. If he'd realised that he was doing Cupid's dirty work he would have left it on her desk for the morning—that way he wouldn't have been witness to her disappointment, her naked vulnerability.

But he had felt uneasy about her, alone in this shabby little flat. If he'd handled things better, perhaps left it to Harriet to invite her to stay, she might have been persuaded to use the guest suite. The message had seemed like an opportunity to try and get her back into the comfort of the house.

'This place needs redecorating,' he said. 'I hadn't realised that it had got so tatty.' He shrugged. 'The younger members of the family like to use it as a base when they're in London.'

'It looks fine to me. I've never had so much room all to myself before.'

Her lack of pretence was refreshing and it suddenly occurred to him that, like his young cousins, she would probably feel more relaxed here. The guest suite might have every luxury an interior designer could imagine, but she'd be exactly that. A guest. Here she could wander about in her dressing gown if she wanted to, completely at her ease. 'Well, if you're happy I'll leave you to catch up on your sleep. I'll see you tomorrow. At about midday.'

'Goodnight, Max. And thank you for bringing the message.'

Jilly waited until she heard his slightly uneven footsteps ringing out on the cobbled courtyard, then she crossed to the door, turned the key and shot home the bolt.

It was a bit late for that, but when she'd turned and seen him standing there, realised just how much of her body was on display, she'd nearly died of embarrassment. And then she'd made it worse by behaving like an aggrieved virgin terrified of being molested. He must think she was an absolute ninny.

Max Fleming was a gentleman. One glance at her legs and then he'd kept his gaze firmly fixed upon her face. It was a bit lowering, actually. Weren't her legs worth a second glance? She swept back the skirt of her dressing gown and looked down at them. It was difficult to tell upside down, but it seemed to her that her thighs were too fat. Oh, hell, who was she kidding? She was too fat everywhere. She'd eaten more chocolate at Christmas than was good for her.

She sighed. She *always* ate more chocolate than was good for her. Maybe she should start running again. Or join a gym. A gym with a sunbed. Because her legs weren't only fat, they were white. When Gemma came home from Florida her slender thighs would be toasted golden brown, along with the rest of her; it would look wonderful with her newly blonde hair.

Jilly swept her hair back from her face and looked in a mirror hanging near the door and wondered what she would look like blonde. Ridiculous. Her brows were too dark to get away with it and then there would be the roots to constantly retouch.

She turned her head. Highlights were a possibility, except she had so much hair that it would take hours. Then she let her hair fall about around her face and comforted herself with the thought that her skin, untroubled by winter sunshine, might not look as glamorous as her cousin's, but it would last longer.

Then she stopped delaying the moment when she would have to read the note left by Max Fleming and finally picked it up.

She'd left her glasses in the bedroom and she held it close to her face and squinted at it, but she didn't need her glasses to see that Richie hadn't left a number other than his office where she could contact him. Or maybe his secretary, if it was the same woman she'd spoken to earlier, hadn't passed it on. Or maybe she was just kidding herself. Maybe Richie wasn't that bothered. Maybe he would think it was a bit of nuisance that she had turned up in London and expected to see him.

On that depressing thought a yawn finally convinced her that it was time to go to bed.

Early to bed, early to rise. Jilly woke to the noise of traffic moving a few streets away and for a moment couldn't think where she was. Then, while she lay in the warm nest of her bed, the important pieces of the previous day gradually formed in her head and fitted together like a jigsaw. She was in London. She'd got a job. And, naturally optimistic, she knew that she'd soon be seeing Richie. A message via his secretary indeed! Who did he think he was impressing?

She glanced at the little alarm clock that she had set to go off at seven. It was still an hour short of that, but she'd been in bed for long enough. She turned it off and flung back the bedclothes. It was too early for the timer on the heating to cut in and for a moment she came close to burrowing back into the warmth and forgetting all about her resolve to take some exercise. But she was wide awake, and no matter how she might try to go back to sleep it just wasn't going to happen.

Instead she leapt out of bed, pulled on her jogging pants and a thick sweatshirt. She was glad she did. It was still dark when she let herself out of the gate and onto the street, but by the time Jilly reached the park she'd noticed from the taxi the day before the sky was streaked with a pink that coloured the frost sparkling on the grass. It was cold, her breath smoking on the frozen air as she pounded along a broad path in front of one of London's grand buildings, but it was beautiful.

Max had risen early too, spent half an hour working out in his own private gym in the basement. He'd been neglecting his exercises, a fact which his leg had been reminding him of for days. He'd spotted Jilly heading across the garden on her way out and was in the kitchen, listening for her, when she returned. He opened the back door and called out to her as he heard the gate.

'I've made some tea, Jilly. Come and have a cup.' She hesitated, breathing heavily, her thick sweatshirt steaming slightly in the cold air. When she turned and walked with every appearance of reluctance towards him, it occurred to him that what had been intended as an invitation might just have sounded more like an order, that, hot and sweaty, she might prefer not to socialise, but didn't feel she could say so. He shrugged, raked his fingers through his damp hair. He was on the steamy side himself. 'Maybe you'd prefer orange juice,' he added, waving towards the fridge as she closed the kitchen door behind her. 'Help yourself.'

'Thanks.' Jilly was breathing too heavily for conversation and her throat was dry, so she poured juice into a glass already on the table. Max Fleming looked very different in a shabby sweat-stained fleece, his dark hair dishevelled, his face flushed from exercise. He looked bigger, more alive somehow, than he had in a suit. But she had been right about those shoulders.

'Where have you been?' he asked.

She looked over the edge of her glass at him. 'I don't know. Some park I noticed yesterday. There was a big house and a pond...'

'That house,' he said, 'is Kensington Palace.' And he nearly laughed out loud at her expression.

'Kensington Palace!' she demanded, horrified. 'Oh, good grief, please don't tell me I've been trespassing?'

'I won't if you don't want me to.' Then, because he saw that this did not reassure her one bit, he said, 'You weren't trespassing, Jilly. Kensington Gardens is a public park.'

'Thank goodness for that.' Her relief was almost comical; obviously Jilly Prescott was a very law-abiding young woman. He'd bet she had never so much as parked on a double-yellow line. 'The only problem is,' she said, 'I was enjoying myself so much that I went much too far.'

'It's easily done,' he said. The innuendo had been unintentional, but if he had hoped to provoke a blush then he would have been disappointed; it completely passed her by. Could she really be that innocent? 'I used to run there myself,' he said, stirring a spoonful of sugar into his tea. 'In the days when I could still run—at least with any style.' She sipped at the juice she had poured herself. 'It was a skiing accident,' he said, answering the unspoken question that hung in air between them.

'I'm sorry.'

'Don't be. I was the lucky one, or so I'm told. I got off with a smashed knee. My wife was killed, as was an old friend of mine…of ours.' Her eyes misted with sympathy and he lifted one corner of his mouth in a cynical smile. 'It's not that bad, Jilly. Really. Just a bit painful when the weather is particularly cold, or damp, which is why I restrict my workouts to the gym these days.' His vague gesture took in the sweat-stained top he was wearing. And he noted with satisfaction first shock, then disapproval at his callous self-concern, drove all trace of sympathy from her face. He had no use for sympathy. He deserved none. 'It's in the basement,' he went on. 'The gym. You're welcome to use it any time. It beats going out in the cold.'

'I like the cold,' she said, stiffly rejecting his invitation. 'But if your knee is painful maybe you should move somewhere where the climate is warm and dry.' Her eyes said a lot more.

'Maybe I should,' he agreed. 'And maybe you'd better go and shower or you'll be late for work.'

So much for a late start. Well, Harriet had warned her. 'Don't worry, Mr Fleming, you won't be overcharged. I'll keep an exact note of my hours for my time sheet.'

'Max,' he reminded her, automatically, as she left. She didn't slam the door, but he had the feeling that it was a close thing. He was still staring after her when Harriet joined him.

'Did we have company?' she asked.

'Just a little tea and sympathy, Harriet.'

She raised a doubting brow in his direction. 'Someone had orange juice.'

'I had the tea and the sympathy.' But he'd soon put a stop to that. 'Jilly preferred juice after her run in the park. What do you think of her?'

'Jilly? She's a nice girl, no airs and graces—'

'Unlike some of the girls Amanda thought suitable?'

'Quite unlike. I don't suppose you've ever seen any of those old Doris Day movies, have you, Max?'

'I can't say that I have. Why?'

'Nothing. It's just that she was a master at the girl-next-door role. The girl-next-door with attitude. There's something about the way Jilly looks you in the eye that puts me in mind of her.' She shook her head. 'Just a silly fancy, I dare say.'

'And what would you say if I told you that she had come to London to be near Rich Blake?'

Harriet stopped clearing the table and gave him her full attention. 'The chap on the television?' He nodded. Her eyebrows did another little tango and then she said, 'Oh, dear.'

'I imagine Doris Day always got her man in the movies?'

'Always. But that was the nineteen-fifties when happy endings were guaranteed. Things are a little different these days and, to be honest, I'm not sure that Rich Blake is anyone's idea of a happy ending. What's her connection with him?'

'They went to the same school, apparently. I don't know how much is fact and how much is fantasy, but

I'm rather afraid that she's in love with him, or thinks she is, which amounts to the same thing.'

'In that case I'd better get in a supply of man-sized tissues. She's going to need them.'

Max shrugged. 'Maybe we're misjudging the man. He had his secretary ring last night and say he'd be in touch soon.'

'His *secretary*? How did she take that?'

He recalled the way the excited glow had gone out of her eyes when she'd realised he hadn't bothered to call her himself. 'You're right. Stock up on tissues, Harriet.'

'It might be kinder to put her on the next train home,' she advised, examining the contents of the fridge.

'Maybe, but she's just about the best shorthand-typist I've ever had work for me, including Laura. I'd be depriving myself of her skills—'

'What is this, Max? A bid for cynic of the year?'

'I'm not a cynic, I'm a realist.'

'Reality hurts.'

'I agree, but there's no way to avoid it and despatching her back to Newcastle would only delay the inevitable. Now that she knows her worth, she'd come straight back to London the minute her cousin returns from holiday.'

It was Friday before Jilly heard from Richie. She'd almost given up hope. She'd called once more only to be told by the girl with the bored voice that he was out and she hadn't tried again. A girl's pride could only take so much.

Max was going through the post, flinging letters at her with a rattle of instructions—'Tell him I'm not interested. Make an appointment for this man. Put this in the diary'—when the phone rang. He picked it up. 'Yes?'

he demanded, then he extended the receiver to Jilly. 'It's for you.'

'For me?'

She half rose, her face flushed with excitement. 'Don't go running off,' he said, despising himself for taking such pleasure in crushing her hopes. 'It's only a woman so you can take it here.'

Reluctantly she lowered herself back into her seat and took the receiver from him. 'This is Jilly Prescott,' she said. Listened briefly. 'Gosh, yes, I'd love to. Will Richie…?' There was a pause. 'But what…?' Then, 'Right, I'll be there. What shall I…?' But the caller, having apparently issued a torrent of instructions, had already rung off. She handed the receiver back to him. 'That was Petra James, Richie's assistant,' she said, with a carelessness that did nothing to disguise her excitement. 'He wants me to take part in a new show he's launching tonight on the television.'

'Tonight? That's rather short notice, isn't it? Did someone drop out at the last moment?'

She flushed furiously. 'There's going to be a party afterwards,' she said, 'and I'm invited.'

'How thrilling for you.' Was that really his voice, weary with boredom, weary with life, pricking at the pleasure she could not stop from bubbling out of her? 'Now can we get on? There's a lot to get through.'

For just a moment there was a flash of something deep in those brown eyes, a moment when he thought he had pushed her too far. Then she carefully chose a newly sharpened pencil from the dwindling pile in front of her and said, 'Of course. I'm sorry you were interrupted.'

Her tightly controlled apology was worse than if she had lost her temper with him. It cut at him. It was simply her obvious delight that Rich Blake had finally bothered to remember her that made him angry—angry that Rich was obviously using her, angry that she should be so happy about it, although why he should care was beyond him.

Except that her eagerness seemed to catch something inside him and squeeze at it, reminding him that there was no one left in the world to light up for him in that way. To glow at just the thought of seeing him, spending time with him.

'No. Forget it.' Disgusted with such self-pity, he stood up somewhat abruptly, tossing the remainder of the post into a tray to be dealt with later. 'Take the rest of the day off, get your hair done, treat yourself to a new dress. If you're going to have your fifteen minutes of fame you'd better be looking your best.' He might make an unlikely fairy godmother, but he did know that if Cinderella Prescott was going to this particular ball she would be needing all the help she could get.

'There's no need, Max…'

'There's every need. You've put in more than enough hours for one week.' As if to make his point he stood up. 'If you'll just call my sister at her office before you go and tell her I'll be taking her out to lunch.' He almost smiled at her stunned reaction. Amanda would be surprised too. Then, as she still seemed determined on protest, 'I mean it, Jilly, I don't want you to be here ten minutes from now.'

And, just to prove his point, he walked from the office leaving her still sitting there with her pencil poised above her notebook, mouth half open in shocked surprise.

CHAPTER FOUR

'So, Max.' Amanda Garland, a glass of spring water in her hand and a thoughtful expression upon her face, regarded her brother with interest. He was too thin, too pale. She worried about him—she worried about him a lot—but knew better than to let it show. 'What exactly do you want?'

'Want?' His smile didn't fool her for a moment. 'Why, nothing but to thank my sister for finding me a secretary with more on her mind than her hair.'

'That's a pity. Jilly Prescott's hair could do with some thought, as could her make-up and her clothes. In fact, if she's going to become one of my girls, I'll have to do something about them.'

'She's fine the way she is. And her hair provides me with endless amusement—it threatens and threatens, but it never quite falls down.'

Amanda wasn't going to argue with him, although she found his defence of the girl interesting. His fascination with her hair…promising. 'Well, that's all right, then. But you could just as easily have picked up the telephone to thank me.'

'I could have,' he conceded, 'but I haven't seen you for a while.'

He thought she would fall for that? 'You haven't seen anyone for a very long time, Max. At least, not socially.' She sipped her iced water and glanced at the menu, although she already knew what she would order. 'I'm glad Jilly suited you,' she said idly.

'She'll do.' He, too, was perusing the menu, avoiding her eyes. 'Where did you find her?'

So, he wanted to know about Jilly Prescott. 'She found me. She wanted to come and work in London and she sent me her CV on spec. Her qualifications were pretty impressive.'

'Even if her hair left a lot to be desired.'

She ignored his sarcasm, and, on the point of ordering a little poached halibut with a rocket salad, she changed her mind. 'I'll have the pheasant with the lentils,' she said. 'We both will.' And looking at her glass with distaste, she added, 'And ask the wine waiter to bring us a bottle of the claret he drinks himself.' Max surrendered his own menu without protest; the knowing look he gave his sister said it all. 'It's cold out,' she said, trying to pass off her choice as nothing more than the need for comfort food. 'I feel the need for something to thicken the blood.'

'Sure,' he said. 'And the earth's flat.'

She hadn't fooled him—well, she hadn't really expected to and her smile admitted as much. 'All right, *you* look as if you could do with something to thicken the blood. Isn't Harriet feeding you?'

'You mean she doesn't give you a weekly report on my calorie intake? Keep you informed as to whether I've eaten up my rice pudding?'

'Harriet Jacobs would never offer you anything as dull as rice pudding.'

'Harriet is a treasure and she's doing her best, Mandy. I just don't have much appetite these days.'

'Well, today you'll eat everything that's put in front of you.'

'Is that right, nanny?' He laughed, then said, 'I'll make a deal with you. I'll match you forkful for forkful.

Let's see just how badly you want me to eat this nour-
ishing stew you've wished upon yourself.'

'You're a rat,' she muttered. He admitted as much
with a graceful gesture. 'Have you any idea how hard I
have to work to keep my figure looking this good?'

'The pheasant was your choice,' he pointed out. 'As
was the claret. And as to your figure, I could quite jus-
tifiably say snap. You too could do with a little less work
and a little more food. You're far too thin.'

'Isn't there a saying involving pots and kettles…?' she
enquired sweetly. 'Besides, after this lunch I'll be the
size of a house.'

'If you eat it. However, since you clearly ordered it
for my benefit rather than your own I imagine you'll
simply pick at it, so your figure, such as it is, is safe.'

'Curves are not stylish, Max—anyway you're wrong.
I intend to eat every mouthful of my lunch, so you'd
better be prepared to keep your end of the deal.' His
smile mocked her. 'And I'll drink my share of the wine.'

'Glass for glass?' Now she'd started this it seemed he
was determined to push her to the limit.

She groaned. 'Have a heart, Max, it is lunchtime. I
have to work this afternoon even if you don't.' Then,
laughing, she surrendered. 'What the heck, it's in a good
cause.' It was worth any amount of pain in the gym just
to see him smile for once, even if it wasn't a full-blown
up-to-the-eyes job.

It was so long since she'd seen him smile, really
smile, let alone heard him laugh. If her suffering was
what it took, then she'd suffer gladly. Except, of course,
it wasn't that simple. Her brother was a complex man
and he never did anything without a good reason. Even
something as simple as taking his sister out to lunch. So

just what was it about Jilly Prescott that had stirred him out of the mausoleum that his house had become?

'I'm glad Jilly suited you,' she said.

'You said.' He was looking out over the harbour, but, although his gaze was fixed upon the expensive yachts moored in the basin, she could tell that his thoughts were turned inwards.

'I was a little worried that she might be too young—' she said, anxious to keep him with her, in spirit as well as body.

He glanced away from the moorings below them. 'Too young for what?' he asked. 'She's a grown woman and one, I might add, who's not afraid of a few curves.'

He'd noticed? She was plain, dowdy, without a shred of style, yet he'd still noticed her old-fashioned hour-glass figure? Amanda shrugged carelessly to disguise the fact that she found the way his mind was running more than a little telling. 'Too young to cope with your bad temper, darling. I did warn her about that. Told her to give as good as she got. I hope she was listening.'

'She was listening, not that I'll admit to a bad temper. I just have a low tolerance of fools and Jilly isn't a fool, at least not at work.'

Ah. 'Well, what she does outside work is hardly any of your business, Max.'

'No...'

'But?'

She saw his face close down and could have kicked herself for her impatience. 'But nothing. You're right. Her private life is none of my business.'

The words sounded right, but somehow Amanda Garland had the feeling that her brother was struggling with that concept. What on earth could Jilly be doing that worried him so much? And why, when some of the loveliest women in London had failed to tempt him out of his hermit-like existence after the death of his wife, was he showing concern for a perfectly ordinary young woman with little to commend her but her shorthand speed?

Jilly couldn't afford a trip to an expensive London hairdresser, let alone the price of a new dress. Besides, she'd seen Richie's kind of television show before. The studio audience wore everything from scruffy jeans and T-shirts to smart casual. And just how dressy could a post-show party be? Everyone else there would have been working all evening and it wasn't as if Richie would be impressed by her efforts—he knew her too well. In fact he'd probably just think it was funny if she tried too obviously to look sexy, and the last thing she wanted was to make him laugh.

But even if she couldn't afford to buy, she could still window-shop and it was good to get out into the fresh air while it was still daylight. There had been precious little chance in the past few days; Max Fleming had scarcely given her time to eat lunch, let alone take a walk in her lunch hour.

It was a fatal mistake, of course. The fluffy sweater with its soft cowl neck was just too much of a temptation—it would look so good with her narrow ankle-length black skirt and her black cross-laced boots.

And, once tempted, it was downhill all the way as she splashed out on a face mask and a new lipstick and nail polish to match the sweater, before dragging herself away from the risk of further extravagance and returning to her little flat to put them all to good use.

It didn't come under the heading of impressing Richie,

she rationalised; this came under the heading of making herself feel good.

On an impulse Max asked the cabbie to drop him at the Bayswater Road entrance to the Broad Walk after he had delivered his sister back to her office, with the intention of walking home through Kensington Gardens.

And he needed a walk after an unexpectedly heavy lunch. It had been a mistake to tease Amanda into having a pudding with the promise that he would if she did. She, at least, had had the sense to stick to some light mousse confection. The pastry of the tarte he had chosen was now sitting like lead in a stomach unused to such excess.

But, as much as exercise, he hoped the sharp air would clear his head, help him to think. He didn't know why he was so uneasy about Jilly Prescott. Maybe it was her innocence, her acceptance of everything and everyone at their face value, that scared him so much. And inviting her to participate in a television game show didn't strike him as the way a friend, a true friend, would choose to get in touch. Especially a game show hosted by Rich Blake.

What on earth did she see in the man? He was loud, cocky and full of himself and couldn't by any stretch of the imagination be described as good-looking, but he had achieved the kind of comet-like stardom that attracted moths to the flame.

And moths got burned.

He probably wouldn't mean to hurt Jilly. He was simply being selfish. Well, Max could understand that. It was a little perverse to blame the man for what he would have once done without thinking himself.

Yet the idea gnawed at him, wouldn't let go.

He had hoped Rich Blake was a complete heel and wouldn't call Jilly again. He was under no illusion that that would have hurt her too, but at least it would have been at long distance and she'd have got the message quickly enough. There was nothing slow about Jilly Prescott. But she was vulnerable, innocent in a way that most women her age were not, and that made him very afraid for her. Although why he should care about a girl he had known for just a few days was a complete mystery.

He had intended to sound out Amanda, perhaps ask her advice, but something knowing in her face had stopped him. He didn't want his sister getting any foolish ideas. He'd better not be getting any foolish ideas himself.

Besides, heartache wasn't fatal. He was living proof of that and he quickened his pace. He had wasted enough time for one day worrying about Jilly Prescott; he doubted she would have thanked him for it, even if she had known.

Nevertheless, when he walked into the kitchen that evening in search of the evening paper and saw her there, he wished he hadn't suggested she buy something special for her evening out.

He had assumed she would be wearing something sexy for the camera, something to catch Rich Blake's eye. Instead she had chosen a softly draped thistledown sweater in the most delicate shade of peach, a shade reflected on those full lips slightly parted now, with just the tip of her tongue showing between her teeth, as she concentrated on threading a needle. She looked soft and cuddly, an armful of comfort, rather like a teddy bear. Yet despite the sudden tightening in his throat, the unexpected lift in his pulse-rate warning that he could quite be easily tempted into an injudicious squeeze himself, her clothes only emphasised her lack of sophistication.

'I thought you'd be long gone,' he said.

She peered over her spectacles, sparing him a momentary glance from beneath long mascara'd lashes, before returning to her thread. 'I should be, but a button came off my coat. Harriet kindly loaned me her sewing basket.'

She was all lit up like a neon sign in Piccadilly Circus, her newly washed hair pinned up in an attempt at sophistication. What she had achieved was a look that suggested one tug of a pin would be all that was needed to bring the whole lot tumbling about her shoulders. In fact he thought she would be lucky if the whole lot didn't descend before she reached the gate. He wanted to tell her not to go. Warn her…

About what? She couldn't be that naive.

But he took out his wallet and extracted a twenty-pound note and offered it to her. 'Just in case,' he said.

Startled, she flashed another glance at him and said, 'In case of what?'

He took her hand and pressed the note into her palm. 'In case you need a taxi home.'

'But—'

But she had no plans to come home that night? Did she think he didn't know?

'Richie will see me home.'

And walk her to her door like a real gentleman? 'I'm sure he will, but you should always have a contingency plan. Things don't necessarily work out the way you expect.'

Harriet was standing behind him and she touched his arm and nodded briefly in approval of his quixotic gesture. 'Your paper is in the study, Max. The fire is lit.'

Ten minutes ago that had been all he had wanted, now his housekeeper's words made him feel about ninety. Another minute and she'd be promising to bring him his slippers.

He was neither old nor an invalid and as if to prove it to himself he took the stairs faster than he had taken them in a very long time, mindless of the pain in his knee.

He'd found his dinner jacket at the back of the wardrobe, dug out a dress shirt and was searching for his studs when he caught sight of himself in the mirror above the dressing table. The gaunt face, the streak of grey glinting in his hair, brought him to an abrupt halt.

What on earth did he think he was doing? Where did he think he was going? The invitations that had once lined the mantel had long since dried up and he hadn't missed them.

So what was he trying to prove?

Just because a pretty young woman with her hormones on fire was standing in his kitchen…

He rubbed his hand over his face. Never again. He'd promised himself that. It was just that tonight…seeing Jilly's flushed and eager face had reminded him that outside the walls of this house was a city vibrating with energy. And that once he had vibrated with it.

He stared at his reflection for a long time and what he saw shocked him. Was that what his sister had seen today? No wonder she worried about him. He was thirty-four years old and he looked nearer fifty.

The studio doorman was expecting Jilly. He ticked her off his list and directed her to the studio. She'd expected Richie to meet her, but he wasn't there, just a group of people who were to take part in the show and a girl with a clipboard who introduced herself as Petra.

'I'll take you all through to the studio in a moment and show you where to sit. Rich will come to your seat at some time during the show and talk to you. Just follow his lead and then, when he invites you down to take part in the show, come down onto the studio floor where I'll be waiting for you.' She smiled briefly. 'Good luck. Now, if you'll follow me.'

They followed her. She glanced at her list and settled each of the contestants in seats throughout the empty auditorium. 'Jilly Prescott?' She glanced at Jilly. 'You're a friend of Rich's, aren't you?'

'That's right.'

'I hope you understand that you'll be taking a chance like everyone else? We can't play favourites.'

'I wouldn't expect you to.'

'Good.' And Petra smiled. 'Just sit here, then. If you get through the first rounds you'll be on set when the show closes, win or lose. It's important that you keep smiling whichever it is and stay where you are while Rich wraps up the show. Don't move until we go off air. That is important. You do understand?'

Did the girl think she was dull-witted, or what? 'I think I can manage that,' she said.

Petra nodded and moved on, still smiling and apparently unaware that Jilly was being more than a little sarcastic.

Jilly only had a few moments to look around at the set, the cameras, before the doors opened and the rest of the eager audience rushed in to grab the best seats. A warm-up man came on to get the audience in screaming mood, although as far as she could see they needed no encouragement, then the show began. She was sitting three rows back. Jilly had phoned her mother to tell her that she would be on television—it would be something to tell Gemma's mother; the pair of them never stopped trying to top one another—and she wondered if anyone she knew had seen her yet.

Richie hadn't. She'd seen straight away that he was focussed one hundred per cent on what was happening in front of the cameras. He was brilliant—not many performers could front a live show and she was so proud of him.

Proud, but disconcerted too. His white-blond hair was accentuated by a deep suntan now, and the glasses had been replaced with expensive contact lenses. This wasn't the boy she had known, the boy she had protected from bullies, given a firm push when he'd been too lazy to get out of his own way.

He began working the audience, picking out contestants apparently at random, chatting to them, revealing something outrageous about them to their apparent embarrassment, although they must have known what was coming. Then, just as she thought he was going to pass her by, he did a double take.

'Jilly?' he said, for all the world as if he had no idea she was in the audience. 'Jilly Prescott?' He made his way past several members of the audience, eased the girl sitting next to her out of her seat and sat down. 'It is really you, pet, all grown up and glamorous?' He didn't wait for an answer, but looked straight into the lens of the camera. 'You won't believe this, but this gorgeous lady used to follow me around at school,' he said. 'She was my first fan. What are you doing now, bonny lass?' he asked, turning on the Geordie charm.

She was almost lost for words. Almost. 'Sitting here, talking to you, Richie,' she said.

'Ooh, cheeky!' he said, and out of sight of the cameras the audience were urged into a long-drawn-out, 'Ooh, cheeky!' as rehearsed by the warm-up man. This was going to be the show's catch-phrase and she'd given him the perfect opportunity to use it.

He grinned at her. 'Nice to see you, Jilly. We'll talk some more after the show.' For a moment she thought he really meant it, that he was going to walk away and leave her there. He was half way out of his seat before he turned back. 'No, wait. I've got a better idea. You can be my last contestant.'

'Won't everyone think it's a fix?' she said, not moving, despite his hand clamped around her wrist. Two, after all, could play at that game.

A momentary flash of surprise was immediately replaced by a big grin as he turned back to the audience. 'Will you?' he demanded. The audience, it seemed, was prepared to be endlessly obliging, but as she descended to the studio floor and saw the look Petra gave her she had the feeling that if she lasted two rounds it would be a miracle.

Max was staring at the screen when Harriet brought in a tray of coffee. 'You'd never think she'd known she was going to be on, would you?' she said, putting the tray on the table beside Max. 'Do you think they rehearsed that beforehand?'

'No, I think Jilly was just being Jilly.'

'I wonder if she'll win something? Maybe it'll be a holiday.'

'Heaven forbid. I don't want her going anywhere until Laura gets back.'

'Have you heard how long that's likely to be?'

'Not yet. Her mother's recovering, but stroke patients can take a long time to get mobile.'

Harriet poured his coffee. 'I shouldn't worry.' He glanced up. 'About Jilly. Thinking about it, he's never going to let her win—the audience would think it was fixed.'

'No. I imagine he has something else in mind for Jilly.' He flicked the remote and the screen went blank.

The games were silly, frantically fast, and the audience was convulsed with hysteria as the contestants fell into booby traps that at first were harmless ball pools, but progressed to tanks of foam and then something that looked unpleasantly like a swamp. Despite the fact that Jilly's hair fell into her eyes the moment she began, and that within seconds she was desperately wishing she'd told Petra she had a pressing engagement that evening, she and three other contestants survived every humiliation that Richie could throw at them.

The next round wasn't so bad, simply a race against time to answer simple multiple choice questions in order to get through a maze. The questions were unbelievably easy but, even so, only the fact that her mother would be watching, would have told all her friends to watch and would be furious with her if she got any of the answers wrong, stopped her from deliberately doing just that in order to escape. Besides, there was no escape. Get the questions wrong and a trapdoor would open and drop her into something that looked very much like custard.

So she answered the simple questions correctly and remembering Petra's injunction to keep smiling she did just that, but at the back of her mind was an insistent little voice promising that Richie would pay for this, a little voice praying that Max wasn't watching.

Max couldn't help himself. The moment Harriet left the room, he turned the television back on. As he had predicted Jilly's hair had begun to slide from its combs the moment the games had begun, her cheeks were flushed and she was grinning fit to bust. He suspected, however, that the grin was fixed and this wasn't how she would willingly choose to spend a Friday evening. But she had agreed to take part and she did it with every appearance of enthusiasm until there were just two of them left to battle it out.

Max found himself sitting on the edge of his seat as Jilly and the other finalist drew lots to choose the two seats that were on centre stage. Both had tanks of some appalling goo fixed above them. Only one of them could win the prize.

Max found himself torn between the hope that she wouldn't win the holiday and disappear into the wide blue yonder, and a horror that she would be subjected to the humiliation of being publicly plastered with thick, brightly coloured gunge.

The audience counted down from ten to one, Rich Blake pulled a huge lever. One of the contestants won the holiday of a lifetime. It wasn't Jilly.

Jilly gritted her teeth and smiled like a trouper. She had seen Petra's smile that second before the goo hit her but refused to give the girl the satisfaction of knowing how angry she was. Instead, she stood there, grinning like an idiot as the sick-green gunk slithered over her face and poured in a thick ooze over her expensive new sweater and favourite skirt, while Richie wound up the show.

Once they were off the air, she promised herself, she would kill him.

When the 'on air' lights went out she waited for him to rush over, apologise. But Richie had other things on his mind and went storming after the floor manager because something hadn't worked quite as smoothly as he thought it should have. It was left to Petra to soothe her. 'Sorry about that,' she said unconvincingly.

Jilly declined to comment. 'Can I clean up, somewhere?'

'Sure. And send me the bill for any damage.' She gave Jilly a card with the production company's name and address on it. Rich Productions. Little Richie Blake had clearly learned fast in the big city. Well, she was learning too.

Twenty minutes later, with her hair wet from the shower and her clothes in a bag, Jilly headed for the exit in a pair of jeans provided by the studio, together with a sweatshirt proclaiming the name of the show in bright letters on the front. Richie cut her off. 'Jilly,' he began, then stopped as he saw her face. He shrugged. 'I'm sorry. It's all a question of luck.'

'Is it?' That smile on Petra's face had suggested otherwise. 'Well, if you'll excuse me, your number one fan is feeling less than...fannish.'

'But we're having a party. I thought you were coming.'

'Like this?'

'Didn't you bring something else to change into? Petra should have warned you that this was a possibility.' The studio was beginning to fill up with women dressed to kill and heading for a temporary bar. One of them was Petra. 'Didn't you warn Jilly what might happen?' Richie demanded.

'Of course I did,' she lied. Jilly hadn't imagined the hostility, then. 'She couldn't have understood.' Oh, she *understood* all right. She was quite capable of recognising a hands-off-he's-mine signal. 'Actually I think the result was just about perfect,' Petra continued. 'The audience loved it.'

'Well, so long as the audience was happy,' Jilly conceded through gritted teeth. 'It's an interesting show, Richie. I'm sure it will be a big hit.'

'You liked it!' She hadn't said that. 'That's my girl. Always a good sport.' He put his arm around her shoulders and turned to those gathering around him, eager to congratulate him on what was undoubtedly going to be a huge success. 'Stand back, everyone, I want to introduce you all to the heroine of the evening. Jilly Prescott. Be nice to her, she's the kid who put me on the road to fame.'

'Really?' Petra said, in the silence that greeted this introduction while everyone looked at Jilly as if she were something from another planet. 'I must have misheard you, Rich. I thought you said she'd put you on the train to London. Someone must have or you'd never have got here.' And suddenly everyone was laughing, especially the stick-thin women in their slashed-to-the-waist dresses that had probably cost more than Jilly earned in a month. That didn't matter. What mattered was that Richie had joined in.

She disengaged herself from his arm. 'Richie, I'm sorry, but I have to go.'

'Go?' He laughed, not believing her. He apparently didn't mind that his assistant had just made her into a laughing stock. 'Don't be silly. Petra, get Jilly a drink.'

'The cars are arriving, Rich. It's time to move on.'

'Are they? Oh, well... We're going on to Spangles, Jilly—'

'That's a nightclub,' Petra interjected, as if she were some idiot up from the sticks who had never heard of the place. Okay, so she *was* an idiot and she *was* up from the sticks, but there couldn't be anyone in the country who hadn't heard of Spangles. It was where the famous partied.

'It's a pity you didn't bring something to change into,' Richie said absently, but his eyes, having flickered over the unflattering sweatshirt and baggy jeans, were already sliding away to the woman next to him, a blonde who was almost wearing a see-through gown with nothing but a few strategically placed sequins to prevent her from being arrested.

Nothing Jilly had in her wardrobe could compete with that. She wouldn't want anything in her wardrobe that would even come close.

'Actually, I have other plans for the rest of the evening.' It wasn't actually a lie. She *did* have plans...they involved making a model of Petra and sticking pins in it. What she had to do now was get out with her pride in one piece, so she gave Richie a quick hug, not that she felt like hugging him, but because she didn't want anyone to think she was sulking.

He didn't try to stop her leaving, but called belatedly after her, 'I'll call you soon, Jilly.'

'Great,' she said, not looking back. 'You do that.' But she wouldn't be holding her breath.

The doorman smiled at her as she left the building. 'Great show. I'm sorry you didn't win the holiday,' he said.

'I came close,' she said, with a wry smile.

'Well, there are no runners up in that game. Can I call you a taxi, miss?'

She thought about the twenty-pound note tucked in her purse 'just in case'. Had Max anticipated something like this?

No, on reflection no one could possibly have foreseen the kind of evening she had been subjected to. At least the other contestants had been willing volunteers...

The doorman was still waiting. 'Thank you, that would be very kind.'

But before he could do that a long black car slid up to the entrance and the driver opened the door for her. 'I was just passing,' Max said, from the rear seat. 'Can I give you a lift?'

Just passing? A likely story. 'In a pig's eye,' she retorted, using his own dismissive phrase back at him. 'You're just trying to save twenty pounds on taxi fares.' But she climbed in beside him and tried to remember how she had felt when she had hailed her first black cab just a few days before. Young, carefree, full of hope. Maybe people aged faster in London, she thought, because she felt years older in the ways of the world than she had then. And since she was a whole lot wiser she was going to pack her bags and go back home where she belonged. 'You saw the whole ghastly thing, I suppose?' she said, leaning back against the soft leather.

'Most of it.'

'And my mother and all her friends—'

'To be fair,' he said quickly, 'they probably thought the whole thing hilarious.'

'The audience certainly enjoyed it,' she agreed.

'But you weren't having quite as much fun as the face-achingly broad smile might have suggested?'

'Fifteen minutes of fame, you said?'

'Apportioned to every one of us, according to Andy Warhol.'

'Just so long as it isn't any more.' She shivered and he took her hand.

'You're cold.' Then angrily, 'How could they let you leave the studio with wet hair on a freezing night like this?'

'Oh, it wasn't their fault. Some girl tried to get me to stay and use a drier.'

'Why didn't you?'

She turned to face him. He was sitting at the far end of the seat, his face in shadow so it was impossible to tell what he was thinking. 'You tell me, Max,' she said. 'You were the one with the car waiting.'

CHAPTER FIVE

'Perhaps it wasn't the best way to resume a relationship when you haven't seen someone for a while,' Max said, after a moment. Then, because it would be a mistake to keep what had happened bottled up, 'Has he changed much?'

'Richie?' Jilly thought about it. There had been changes. He'd been wearing expensive, if hideously bright, clothes for the show, a sunbed tan disguised his more usual pallor and the spectacles with the sticking plaster had disappeared, but those were superficial things. She remembered the way Petra had controlled him, the way he had let her. 'Not as much as he thinks he has,' she said at last. 'I used to chase after him, making sure he was where he was supposed to be, had his homework, had a pen. The only difference as far as I can see is that I did it for free and now he pays a high-powered assistant to do it.' She managed a smile. 'Actually I think she'd probably do it for free as well, if he asked her.'

So. Sweet little Jilly was capable of something as downright human as jealousy, was she? 'What's she like? His assistant.'

'Gorgeous. Red hair, a figure like a stick insect and eyes of such an improbable turquoise that I suspect coloured contact lenses are involved.'

'That's better.'

'What?'

He grinned. 'Bitchiness is always a hopeful sign. And you almost laughed.'

'Only at myself. I've made a real fool of myself, haven't I?'

'Hardly that, Jilly. He's just moved on, left you behind. It happens.'

'Well, he had no right to leave me behind. If it wasn't for me he'd still be running a disco outfit for the local youth club.'

'Oh, come on—'

'Don't patronise me!' Her eyes flashed at him, bringing him crashing to a halt. She was angry, really angry. 'I'm not some silly little girl with a crush on some bloke who smiled at me once in the school yard. Richie Blake didn't move on, Max. I pushed him. He admitted as much tonight. ''Be nice to her,'' he said, ''she's the kid who put me on the road to fame.''' Then he had allowed Petra to make a joke out of it. Her face burned as she remembered.

'Then I don't understand. Why aren't you still there? Didn't you say that Rich is throwing a party to celebrate his new show?'

'Yes, I did.' She made a gesture encompassing her clothes. 'I thought it was going to be a casual thing at the studio.'

'It wasn't?'

'No, it wasn't. Petra forgot to tell me that they were all going on to some fancy nightclub. Petra—'

'The glamorous assistant?'

She nodded. 'Petra was supposed to tell me, so that I would bring something suitable to change into after the show.'

'But she didn't.'

'Every other woman there was practically naked. One

of them wore a dress slashed to here…' she jabbed dramatically at her waist '…and another one was almost wearing something that would have got her arrested but for a few well-placed sequins. And—'

'I get the picture,' he said, catching her wildly gesticulating hands, holding them.

She stopped, looked up at him and was suddenly shaken by a long, shuddering sob. 'Oh, damn!' she said. 'Damn! I promised myself I wouldn't do this—'

Max wasn't quite sure how he came to be holding her, but somehow his arms were around her and her tears were soaking through his sweater to his shirt so that he could feel them against his skin. And her whole body was shaking as she was racked with sobs while he murmured all kinds of platitudes, none of which was the slightest bit of use.

'Oh, God!' She pulled back so suddenly that she took him by surprise. 'I can't believe I'm crying!' She rubbed angrily at a tear-stained cheek with the heel of her hand. 'It's not as if I *care*—'

Just who did she think she was kidding? She cared all right. 'Hey, calm down,' Max said, offering her a handkerchief as she smeared her mascara where it had run with her tears. 'What you need is—'

'If you dare to tell me what I need is a nice cup of tea, Max, I promise I'll hit you,' she warned.

A cup of tea was exactly what she needed, but, since he didn't have one to offer, he leaned forward and opened the drinks cabinet. 'Brandy,' he said, taking out a miniature and sharing it between two glasses. 'It'll warm you up,' he said, pressing a glass into her hand. 'It'll warm us both.' Then he glanced at his watch. Ten-thirty. The night had scarcely started. 'Where are they going? Do you know?'

'Spangles,' she said as she sipped the brandy, then spluttered as the heat hit the back of her throat.

'Of course.' He considered the possibilities. 'It's not too late, you know. You could go home, change and join them.'

'Walk into some flashy nightclub on my own?' She swallowed more of the brandy. 'I don't think so. Besides—' He waited. She shrugged. 'I said I had other plans for the evening.'

Of course she had. And she'd walked out with her head high. Not that anybody would have believed her. Max Fleming stared into the brandy pooled in the bottom of his glass for a long moment. Then he raised it to his lips and swallowed it. 'Did you say what other plans?'

'No.'

And they hadn't been sufficiently interested to ask, Max could tell. 'I haven't been to Spangles for a long time. I wonder if it's changed much?' Jilly didn't answer—well, he hadn't really expected her to. 'I was only thinking this evening that it's too long since I made an effort…that I should get out a bit more…' He opened another miniature and shared it between their glasses. 'Dancing is such good exercise, too. Just what the doctor ordered.' He swallowed a mouthful of spirit. 'How long would it take you to change, Jilly?'

'Change?'

'Into something suitable for a nightclub.'

'Oh, no, Max. I couldn't—' He didn't answer her, but continued to regard her thoughtfully, wondering what she would look like in a dress slashed to the waist. His imagination, he discovered, was in full working order and his libido was catching up fast. 'I don't possess a dress that could even come close to what those other women were wearing tonight, Max,' she protested.

'I've got a room full of dresses,' he began, then realised what he had said. What he was offering. Charlotte's clothes had remained untouched since she died. But Charlotte would have been the first to offer…would have been the first to say he should do this… The car slid to a halt at the front gate. 'Wait here,' he told the driver. 'I'll need you for the rest of the night. Come on, Jilly. You are about to put Miss Petra Smartypants' nose out of joint.'

'I can't. You can't—'

'I can and I will. And so can you.' And, taking her wrist, he led her into the house and straight up the stairs.

'Max!' Her protest went unheeded and his grasp was not to be shaken off until he threw open a door, snapped on the lights and walked in. It was not, as she feared, his bedroom, but a large dressing room.

The dressing table was laid out with small pots of expensive cosmetics, silver-backed brushes, tortoiseshell combs. Max released her, crossed the room and pushed open a door, and for a moment he stared into a white and gold bathroom that made the cloakroom on the ground floor look, well, ordinary.

He turned back, saw her staring. 'I was just checking, but everything seems to be…towels…' Abruptly he turned his attention to the closets, flinging back the doors to reveal racks of clothes. Beautiful clothes. Hand-stitched designer clothes from the greatest fashion houses in the world.

'This was your wife's room,' she said, and it wasn't a question. 'Her clothes.'

He turned to her. 'Does that bother you?'

'Doesn't it bother you?' she asked as he flipped through the rack as if he were at an Oxford Street sale, glancing at and then discarding dresses that glittered, fabrics that glowed.

'Yes, actually, it does. It's a criminal waste leaving them hanging here like this. I shouldn't think Charlotte ever wore an evening gown more than once.'

That would explain why she had so many... 'That's not the point, Max. You can't dress me up in your wife's clothes and parade me like some—'

He finally found what he was looking for. Slinky, exquisitely understated, the gown he removed from the closet was a stylish slither of slipper satin in almost exactly the same shade of peach as the sweater she had been wearing. He held it against her, draping it across her shoulder, fanning the material out, then, as if suddenly registering her protest, he looked up.

'Some what?' he asked, his brows drawn down in a slightly puzzled expression. She didn't believe that expression. He knew exactly what she meant.

Jilly swallowed, hard. 'You just can't. I can't.'

'Charlotte wouldn't object, Jilly—in fact she'd think the whole thing rather a lark—'

'Would she?' She touched the smooth velvet softness of the gown and wondered what it would feel like against her skin.

As if he could read that in her face, Max lifted the hem of the skirt and stroked it against her cheek. It was sensuous, thrilling, wickedly seductive. 'Tell me, Jilly, if you were wearing this,' he murmured in a voice that was little more than a provocative echo of the touch of the fabric, 'how do you think the lady with nothing between her and decency but a few sequins would feel?'

'Cheap,' she said, without a second's hesitation.

'And?'

'Jealous?' she offered.

'Maybe,' he said. Then he lifted a pair of heavy lids so that his dark eyes met hers, held them in the searchlight of a gaze that seemed capable of reading her innermost secrets, every hidden desire. 'Wouldn't you like to find out?'

Jilly was human enough to want that, but she knew when something was utterly impossible. She was about to tell him so, to thank him, but tell him that it really would be better if she packed her bag and went home. But as she gathered herself, searched for the words, she saw that he already knew what she would say, saw a momentary flash of something raw, an unsuspected pain he usually kept deeply hidden beneath a veneer of cynicism and irritability. In a rare flash of insight she realised that he needed her to take the dress, to accept his help, far more than she needed to take it.

She tried to speak, but her mouth was suddenly dry. She swallowed. 'It…it might not fit,' she said.

His smile was slow in coming, but it was worth waiting for. 'Shall we see?' While she was still trying to work out what *that* meant, he slipped his arm about her waist and moved closer, taking her right hand as if they were about to dance one of those old-fashioned dances where a man held a woman close, and for a long moment he held her so that she could see the pulse beating in his throat, smell the warmth of his skin, the faint aroma of brandy lingering on his mouth. Then he looked down at her with eyes like rain-washed slate. 'Trust me,' he said, his voice suddenly coming through cobwebs. 'The dress will fit.'

Jilly's heart was pounding from the unexpected contact, the way his hand was cradling hers, the touch of his arm about her waist. The way he was looking at her. 'Oh,' she said. 'Well, good.'

'How long will it take for you to get ready?'

'Half an hour?' she offered hoarsely, looking up into a face as close as that of a lover, close enough to kiss her, close enough to touch his lips to her throat...

'Make it twenty minutes.'

Jerked back into her senses, she stepped back. 'My hair takes that long.'

Her hair, left to its own devices, had dried in a mass of tiny waves and without thinking Max reached out, scooped a handful of it from her neck before letting it fall through his fingers. He didn't think there was a comb made that was capable of restraining it for more than five minutes. 'Leave it loose,' he said. Then, 'You'll find everything you need here. Help yourself. I'll be in the study when you're ready.' Then he turned rather abruptly on his heel and walked from the room, closing the door firmly behind him.

Jilly swallowed hard. Something had just happened. Max Fleming had held her for no more than thirty seconds, yet something had happened. And then his fingers had brushed against her neck setting off a vibration, something not quite a shiver but more than a pulse that seemed to race over her skin, setting it on edge, raising the fine down so that every part of her seemed suddenly more aware, more alive.

She lifted her arm, stared at her wrist where she could still feel the imprint of his fingers against her skin like a bracelet. She flexed her wrist, rubbed at it, but the sensation did not go away and after a moment she turned and walked slowly across to the dressing table.

Silver-backed brushes were laid ready for a woman who would never use them again, a crystal tray contained every conceivable kind of hairpin set out in neat rows. Bottles of scent, names that she had only ever read about in expensive magazines, stood in their boxes to preserve them from the light. Only one exquisite bottle, engraved with the letter C upon the stopper, stood apart. C for Charlotte? Curiosity drove her to open it and lift it to her nose. It was like nothing she had ever encountered on a chain-store perfume counter. Exotic, spicy, exciting. She dabbed a little on her wrist and then wished she hadn't as the heavy fragrance rapidly expanded in the heat of her pulse and she raced to the bathroom desperate to wash it off. Max had invited her to make use of everything she wanted. She was almost certain that invitation had not included his wife's special scent.

Her face, reflected in the harsh light over the bathroom mirror, was a shock. Mascara all over the place, blotchy cheeks. What on earth had she been thinking of? Who on earth would want to kiss her looking like that? And what was Max thinking of? It would take more than cosmetics and an elegant dress to make her presentable. It would take a miracle.

But if it needed a miracle to transform her, then Charlotte Fleming's dressing room was clearly the place for it. Max was right. Everything a woman might ever desire was here. She started with make-up remover and moved on to the shower. By then the blotches had disappeared and, wrapped in a towel she returned to the dressing table and set to work.

And it was barely twenty minutes later that she turned to pick up the dress Max had chosen for her and lifted, as he had, the smooth fabric to her cheek.

She had no objection to the idea of swanning into a nightclub looking a million dollars—and in this dress she could scarcely help it. Just the thought of the likely effect on Petra was enough to make her day, her week even. Quite possibly her year. Because it wasn't the woman in the nearly-there dress who was her rival—it was Petra. Nearly-there might have her moment, but it was Petra who organised Richie's life these days and he did need someone to organise his life, hold his hand, reassure him.

No matter how many semi-clad models draped themselves invitingly about him, he would always need someone to turn to in moments of crisis, someone to hold his hand, and Petra was clever enough to recognise the only real opposition to her power would come from the girl from back home who knew his every weakness, from whom he had no secrets.

And she had let the woman walk all over her, push her out. Had even contemplated walking away and leaving her to it. Was she mad? Why was she hesitating for even a second?

Because things like this didn't happen to girls like her, that was why. She had no illusions about herself. She was an ordinary girl, from an ordinary home in a very ordinary little town in the north-east of England. But as she stepped into the dress, smoothed it over her body, turned to check her reflection from every angle, she knew that in a dress like this, in the arms of a man like Max Fleming, it would be very easy to forget that.

As Max fitted cuff-links into his shirt he was calling himself every kind of idiot. What on earth did he think he was doing? Delivering this girl into the arms of a man who did not value her would probably do nothing but hurt her.

But it was too late now for second thoughts.

He straightened his tie, slipped on his dinner jacket and regarded his reflection for the second time that evening. What would they see, all those curious people who would raise their eyebrows at his re-emergence on the social scene? Nothing. Because there was nothing to see. He was a hollow man. Empty. He reached for his cane and then in a gesture of irritation he flung it aside. The only prop he needed right now was a drink. But as he reached for the decanter he knew that wouldn't help, either. He would be better occupied organising a table at Spangles.

He had just replaced the receiver on the telephone when the door behind him opened. For a moment, one terrible moment as the scent she was wearing reached out to spark a hundred, a thousand memories, he couldn't bring himself to turn around, terrified of what he might see.

'Max?'

Her soft voice, elusive accent, so different from Charlotte's well-rounded vowels, snapped him out of the nightmare and he spun around. This was no ghost. For height and figure, she was close enough, but in every other way she was the very antithesis of Charlotte.

Her dark hair billowed in a cloud around her face, where his wife had been fair. Soft brown eyes regarded him uncertainly instead of that unforgettable forget-me-not blue. Charlotte had been the classic English rose, while Jilly had an altogether earthier, warmer look to her. There was no danger here. But, even so, he had been right about the dress. It was a perfect foil for her dark colouring, clinging to her white skin before swirling around her legs, displaying their long, elegant shape as she moved. Had he thought of her as an ordinary young woman?

He had been wrong. She was not ordinary. She would turn heads tonight; it would take a man without feelings, without imagination, without a heart not to respond to her. Even a man without a heart might feel an echo of some dimly remembered ache…

'I told you the dress would fit,' he said brusquely.

'What a pity you didn't think about shoes,' she responded sharply. But he heard the disappointment catch in her throat; she'd expected a polite compliment at least. But polite would not be enough. More was beyond him. Then she lifted her chin a little and her soft mouth trembled on a smile. He avoided it by looking at her feet. 'Your wife had smaller feet than me. I managed with a pair of silver sandals,' she said. 'Just don't take me hiking.'

'I won't do that, but you'll need a coat. There are furs, a silver fox that would look perfect—'

'I couldn't wear a fur.' Her mouth no longer trembled as she dared him to attempt to persuade her. He knew better than to try, but she raced on just in case he made the attempt. 'I found a long velvet coat.'

'Whatever. If you're ready, I suggest we go.'

'Max, look, you don't have to—'

'Try and stop me,' he said, cutting off her words and crossing to the door, opening it for her. A few minutes earlier he had been wishing this offer unmade. Having seen her, he couldn't possibly back out. 'The car is waiting.'

After the tiniest hesitation she walked past him and picked up a small beaded evening bag from the hall table, then waited obediently while he held the pale silvery velvet coat for her. It reached the floor and looked stunning on her, although this too smelled faintly of Charlotte's scent. It was a unique fragrance that he'd had blended for her as a birthday gift and she'd worn it always. At least she had until she had given up trying to love him. Given up the pretence that she ever could.

He stepped back, distancing himself from the painfully familiar scent, and put on his coat, looped a white silk scarf around his neck before heading for the door.

Her voice stopped him. 'Don't you need your cane?'

He finally managed a smile. 'I don't think the cane would be such a good idea. The whole point of this exercise is to pique Mr Blake's interest. We won't do that if I look like some old crock you've taken pity on.'

'You don't look like any kind of crock!' she declared.

'Don't I? Well, appearances can be deceptive. But if my leg gives me any trouble I promise I'll put my arm around you for support. That will really give him something to think about.' He opened the door and ushered her through. 'Your carriage awaits, my lady,' he said, with a sketch at a bow. 'Cinderella *shall* go to the ball.'

'Oh, right,' she said. 'And who are you supposed to be? Prince Charming?'

'Isn't that supposed to be Rich Blake's role?' he replied, offering her his arm, then leading her down the path towards the waiting car.

She pulled a face. 'Richie? He wouldn't know how. But if you're not Prince Charming, who are you?'

He tutted. 'You don't recognise me without the cane. Or should I say wand?'

She laughed. 'You're my fairy godmother?'

'P-lease! God*father*.'

She laughed again. 'You look more like the demon king,' she said, laying her head back against the soft leather of the seat as the car sped through the dark London streets.

'Wrong story.'

She turned her head to look at him. 'Maybe.' But, with his silver-streaked hair, saturnine face, dark eyes, Max Fleming looked thoroughly dangerous. And, despite his big-time television career, Richie Blake looked like a callow boy alongside him.

There was a huddle of photographers waiting outside the club, a sure sign that serious celebrities were inside. Max climbed out and reached for her hand. She looked so nervous that he gave it a reassuring squeeze. 'Big smile, Jilly. They won't bite.'

'Won't they? What will they do?'

'Take your photograph, make you famous.' He raised his brows. '*Won't* Petra be cross?' he said, inviting her to join him in a smile.

Having decided that he was kidding her, she relaxed and the smile came naturally. 'Absolutely livid,' she said.

They were halfway across the pavement before one of the photographers recognised him. 'Mr Fleming?' Jilly hesitated, glanced towards them, but his hand at her back kept her moving. 'Max Fleming?' the man repeated, louder this time so that, by the time they had reached the doorway and he turned to acknowledge the greeting and, coincidentally, present them with a perfect view of Jilly, there was a most satisfactory barrage of flashlight. 'I haven't seen you for a while, Mr Fleming,' the first photographer persisted.

'I've been busy. Who's brought you all here this evening?' As if he didn't know.

'No one you know. Who's the young lady?' He didn't answer them but glanced down at Jilly as there was another volley of flashlight. 'Is she an actress, sir? Or a model? What's the story?'

'Who said there's a story?' Then he grinned at them just to make sure they knew he was kidding. 'We're just two good friends having a quiet night out.'

'And how long have you been good friends, Mr Fleming?'

But he'd given them more than enough to raise their interest, and instead of answering he turned and ushered Jilly inside the club. It might have been a couple of years since he'd been there but inside he was greeted like an old friend. Jilly, having parted with her coat, rejoined him. 'Will I really have my picture in the newspapers?' she whispered as they were shown to a table.

'Probably. Unless something really interesting happens this evening.'

'Like what?'

Like someone hitting Rich Blake, very hard. The man had taken a bottle of champagne from one of the waiters and was shaking it furiously, egged on by his companions. As they watched, it erupted with a torrent of bubbles that showered everyone. They didn't seem to mind. The *maître* followed Max's gaze. 'Mr Blake is celebrating a successful new television show and is eager to share his good fortune,' he murmured.

'Mr Blake will get himself into trouble if he doesn't behave himself,' Jilly said primly.

Max glanced down at her. 'Just high spirits, darling.' Then he turned back to Marco. 'I'd prefer he didn't share it with us. As far away from them as you can, if you please, Marco.'

'Of course, Mr Fleming. As soon as you rang I had a table put near the dance floor for you.'

Jilly came to a halt. 'But I thought we were—'

'Have a little patience, Jilly,' he said, following the *maître* as he led the way through the crowds of late night revellers and settled them at a small table for two in one of the most desirable locations in the room. But Jilly's gaze was still fixed on Rich Blake and Max touched her hand to draw her attention back to himself, at least for the moment. 'You had other plans, remember? You had no idea I would bring you here.' Then, rather more irritably, 'And don't stare. Blake'll notice you soon enough.'

And then what would he do? Simply surrender her and walk away? Common sense suggested that it would be the wise thing to do. But there wasn't much about this evening that could be described as wise, or sensible. A wise man would have chosen not to get involved. A sensible man would have encouraged Jilly Prescott to pack her bags and catch the next train home, no matter what the personal inconvenience. There would be nothing but heartbreak for her here, he was certain.

But since he hadn't done either of those things, instead plunging the girl into a harebrained adventure for motives he didn't understand himself, he had a responsibility to do his best to ensure that it at least had the outcome she was hoping for. But was displaying Jilly to her best advantage, and then leaving her to get on with the results, responsible? And suppose Rich Blake didn't bite? How would she feel then?

As he watched the man's loud antics, saw the way he was pawing a scantily clad girl who had just landed in his lap, Max suspected that he would consider a bird in the hand more than enough to cope with for one night. And then there was the pretty redhead who was looking decidedly proprietorial. Jilly would certainly have her work cut out to make an impression.

'Is this satisfactory, Mr Fleming?'

'Perfect, Marco. If you'll just send over a bottle of Bollinger.' He turned to Jilly. 'Are you hungry?' She shook her head. 'Nothing else.' Marco bowed slightly and departed. For a moment they sat in awkward silence,

Jilly's eyes fixed upon the noisy scene on the far side of the room. 'I wish—'

'What?'

She stared down at the table. 'I wish that I hadn't come. This isn't me.'

Maybe not, but it would become her quickly enough when Blake noticed her. 'They say you should be careful what you wish for, just in case it comes true.'

She turned and glared at him. 'Actually, I don't remember wishing to be here.'

'Not out loud, maybe. But in your head—'

'And you're a mind-reader? In that case you'll know exactly what I'm thinking now.'

Her irritation was the result of disappointment and he could understand that. But what exactly had she expected? That Rich Blake would drop the armful of curves he was holding and rush to clasp her to his manly chest? Well, his chest anyway. Max could be just as bitchy as Jilly. But even in fairy tales these things took time.

'Well?' she demanded.

'Would you like to go across and join the party? Since you know him, were invited, it would be perfectly in order.'

'Do you think he'd actually notice?'

'He does seem to be fully occupied at the moment.'

'Yes, he does, doesn't he?'

But since he had raised her expectations, brought her here, he would do something about that. 'Have a glass of champagne,' he said as the waiter arrived.

'Why?'

'Because everything looks better after a glass of champagne.' He placed a glass in her hand. Maybe with a drink inside her she would begin to relax a little, forget

Blake for long enough to begin to enjoy herself. And it was essential that she forget about him, enjoy herself, if she was going to attract notice.

'Why on earth did I ever agree to this?'

'Fortune favours the bold, Jilly,' he said, touching his glass to hers. 'So, tell me, just how bold are you feeling?'

CHAPTER SIX

JILLY emptied her glass in a gesture at once bold and reckless. 'You think I'm mad, don't you?'

He refilled her glass. 'Of course you're mad. There's nothing sane about love, believe me, I know.'

She turned and looked at him then. Love? Who'd said anything about love? Then she realised that he was staring at her—or rather the dress she was wearing. 'You must have loved your wife very much.'

'Must I? To be honest I've never been able to decide whether I loved her too much, or not enough.' Max drained his glass and stood up rather too quickly. Pain scythed through his knee, a permanent jog for his conscience, a reminder of the consequences of listening to a selfish heart. 'Come along, Jilly, enough of this maudlin nonsense. Let's dance.'

Jilly stared up at him.

Beads of sweat had broken out on his forehead and there was a whiteness about his mouth that hadn't been there a moment before. 'Are you sure? You don't have to go through with this—'

'I wasn't planning on giving a demonstration of the tango. There's no room.'

'I just meant—' she began, then stopped. Tango? He thought she was talking about dancing? About his leg? Was it physical pain that had caused the reaction she had witnessed?

'If I promise you that I won't fall over, will you risk it?' he said impatiently. Then he looked down. 'See?

One leg on each side and they both work most of the time. A gentle steer around the dance floor is just what the doctor ordered.'

Somehow his smooth drawl didn't quite convince her and the dance floor was crowded, certainly not the place for anything very gentle, but Max Fleming was not a man to argue with so she didn't try. And painfully aware that, by her own standards, she was not behaving any better than Richie, she apologised.

'I'm sorry, Max.' And to prove it she made herself smile.

That smile nearly broke Max. Jilly was clearly wishing that she hadn't allowed him to talk her into this, wishing that she were safely tucked up in bed where nothing could hurt her. Maybe she should be. No one enjoyed being hurt. 'I didn't say this would be easy, Jilly, but if you want something badly enough, you fight for it. That way you keep your self-respect, the knowledge that you couldn't have done any more.' Why was he telling her that? Hadn't he learned anything?

Jilly shifted awkwardly, glanced down at her dress. 'I feel a little overdressed for someone seeking simple self-respect.'

'You look lovely. Beautiful. I'm the envy of every man in the room.'

She glanced up and for a moment thought he meant it. 'Idiot,' she muttered, but despite the throbbing music Max heard her.

'On that we are in total agreement,' he said, assuming she meant him, then took her arm, eased her to her feet before she could raise any further objections and moved with her onto the dance floor. It was hot and crowded, with barely room to move, so holding her close was scarcely a matter of choice. Not that she was objecting.

They were attracting attention all right, but it was she who was attracting the envious looks. If only they knew.

'You were right, Max,' she said as they squeezed into the crush and she began to dance, at first self-consciously, holding herself stiffly even though his touch was feather-light at her back.

'Right?'

'There's no room to tango.'

'Well, thank heaven for that. I'd look really stupid with a rose between my teeth.'

Jilly finally laughed, relaxed a little so that Max could hold her closer, close enough to discern that all that stood between his hand and her skin was a shimmer of peach satin. The knowledge slipped into his brain like a virus and one by one his senses were switched on, warmed up and became fully engaged.

Maybe it was because they had been unused for so long that they were extrasensitive now. He just couldn't get the idea out of his mind that her skin would feel exactly like the satin: smooth and soft, warm to the touch. And as he let his hand slide lower to her waist little shocks of pleasure bombarded the sensory nerves at the tips of his fingers, raising the fine hairs on his skin. His hold tightened as he drew her closer. 'Put your arms around my neck,' he murmured. Jilly simply stared at him. 'I thought you wanted to make Blake jealous.'

Richie? Who in their right mind would be thinking about Richie at a moment like this? Jilly pulled herself together. 'Richie won't notice.'

'Oh, he will. He has.' Max, a head taller than Jilly, could see him now dancing with his sequined partner. He had already looked in their direction. And then looked again.

Jilly, for a moment awkward in the intimate embrace

of a man she barely knew, a man she worked for, suddenly discovered there was something special about dancing close to the kind of man that midnight dreams were made of. Richie, despite his celebrity status, was ordinary, a boy she'd known all her life. Max was different. There was a careless arrogance about him that came from centuries of breeding, centuries of knowing that you were special.

Everything about him was different. The freshly starched scent of his shirt, the smooth, expensive touch of his dinner jacket beneath her hand, and whatever cologne or aftershave he had used was so subtle that she could scarcely say whether the scent was real or whether she was imagining it. Putting her arms about his neck, laying her head against his chest was by no means a penance, and her lips softened into a smile as he put both hands about her waist and pulled her closer so that she was listening to the slow thud of his heart overlaying the sensuous beat of the music. Two hours ago she'd been enduring hell at the hands of Rich Blake; quite suddenly she was being transported to heaven.

Max shifted his hold slightly, so that his hands rested on the soft curve of her hips. It was heaven and it was hell too. Like the pain when frozen fingers began to thaw, and for just a moment he felt dizzy…

Her scent seemed to fill him up. That tormenting scent that had been solely Charlotte's and yet on Jilly's skin was subtly different, the way he had always imagined it should be…

Then the music changed to something more earthy, a primitive beat that seemed to vibrate through her, so that she eased away from him and even though he didn't want to let her go he had no choice. And yet this, too, was perfect as she closed her eyes, letting the music seep into her mind, fill her with its rhythm, her dark hair swinging, glistening in the lights, so that each strand seemed to reflect a different colour.

For a moment he simply stood and watched as she lifted her slender arms, moving them in time with the rhythm while her hips swayed as if she were alone somewhere with just the music inside her head and there was no one to see the way the delicate cloth of her gown clung to her body, revealing far more than she could ever have realised. And he knew then that he wanted her. Wanted her to do this for him alone.

But already she was attracting attention. Hot eyes, including those of Rich Blake, had turned in her direction and Blake's eyes had narrowed, his face creased in a frown as he struggled to reconcile what he was seeing with what he knew. Another minute and he would realise who she was. He wouldn't quite believe it at first, think it was some mistake, an illusion of the light, but the idea would have lodged inside his head and eventually he would have to squeeze through the crush to convince himself that he was wrong.

Except, of course, he wouldn't be wrong and Jilly wouldn't be able to disguise her pleasure at seeing him.

Indignation took Max by the throat, welled up from some deep visceral part of him and revolted. Rich Blake would never value any woman who came to him that easily. He mustn't get that close. Not tonight. Tomorrow, he would see her in the paper and know he had not been mistaken and, his interest thoroughly aroused, he would come looking for her. But Blake wouldn't have her, not if he had anything to do with it. Not yet. First he would have to learn what it was to desire a woman, to yearn for her, to treasure her, to feel the bite of jealousy, love her enough to be prepared to lose everything for her…

'Jilly...' She opened her eyes; they were huge, very dark in the subdued lighting of the club.

Her mouth was soft and inviting, her lips slightly parted as, brought out of the depths of the music, she stared up at him. He stretched out a hand to her and she came to him so easily, her fingers placed on his, her arm on his arm as she looked up with sudden concern. 'Max, are you all right?'

No. He was not all right. He was anything but all right. As he bent over her there was a fierce pulse pounding in his head, an ache gathering in the pit of his body that intensified as he bent to murmur in her ear, his face brushing against the fine, pale skin of her temple.

'Let's get out of here, Jilly.'

'Go?'

His gaze was fastened to her mouth as they rounded on the word. Soft, peachy, sunshine and laughter lips. His own mouth was throbbing with an urgent, almost overwhelming desire to succumb to temptation and taste them. That would really give Rich Blake something to think about. Maybe he should do just that.

'You mean leave?'

'Now,' he said urgently, before he forgot himself entirely. Then, because she was still slightly confused by this sudden change of tactics, 'Trust me, Jilly. I'm your fairy godfather, remember?' Just as long as he didn't forget that was all he was supposed to be, they'd be fine. He tightened his grip on her fingers and headed for the stairs. 'Just imagine that the clock has struck twelve and the car is about to turn into a pumpkin.'

'But Richie—'

Dear God, did she never think of anything but Rich Blake? 'He'll wait,' he snapped.

She came to an abrupt halt, forcing him to do the same. 'My bag,' she said. 'I left my bag on the table.'

'Oh.' Then, 'Leave it, it'll make a change from glass slippers.'

'I can't do that!'

'There can't be anything valuable in it.'

'The bag is valuable. It belonged to your…' His sharp look stayed the words on her tongue. 'And there's the twenty-pound note you gave me in it.' She gave him a sideways look as she made a determined detour via the table and he was forced to follow her while she retrieved it. 'Just in case.'

He supposed he deserved that. 'Get your coat, Jilly,' he said, easing her in front of him as they reached the wide-sweeping stairs, determined that she shouldn't be sidetracked by anything else. She ran lightly up the steps while he paused at the bottom, pain stabbing suddenly through his knee. He bit back a grimace and then more slowly began to follow her, but halfway up as he put his weight on his injured leg it crumpled beneath him and he stumbled, grabbed for the rail. 'Damn!' The word escaped him. Then, 'Go on, Jilly. I'll be right behind you,' he urged as she stopped, looked back. For a moment he just hung on willing his wretched leg to work. It refused point-blank to co-operate and he sank onto the step.

'Someone's been enjoying himself,' a girl said as she swept past them on her way down into the club and her companion laughed.

Jilly, furious at such stupidity, glared at their self-satisfied, moronic backs, then joined Max on the step, sitting beside him, taking his hand between hers as she saw the whiteness about his mouth. He was in pain, she saw. But he was not about to admit it.

'Idiot,' she said, leaning her head against his shoulder as if they were sitting there because they wanted to and for no other reason.

'Say that again and I'll fire you.'

'In a pig's ear...'

'Eye,' he corrected, managing a smile. 'Okay, okay, I'm an idiot, but if you say I told you so, I'll—'

'Yeah, yeah, you're all talk. Put your arm around me, Max.' She didn't wait, but lifted his arm and wriggled beneath it. Then she smiled up at him as she snuggled against him.

'People will think we're in love,' he said.

'That's the general idea. It's got to be better than them thinking we're drunk.'

'Yes.' He turned and stared at her for a moment. Her face was inches from his, her eyes filled with concern, her lips slightly parted on an overbite that had never been properly corrected.

Then, 'What?' she asked. 'What are you thinking?'

Her mouth was a warm invitation. 'I'm thinking that we could be a whole lot more convincing,' he said.

Jilly's throat dried. 'How?'

'Like this.' And he kissed her. Like some lost-in-love boy at a party, he let her head fall back over his arm and he kissed her. He had not imagined the warmth—it seeped into him like some healing balm, spreading through him, heating him. He had not imagined the sweetness. What almost blew his mind was the unexpected way she kissed him back, as if she had been waiting for this moment all her life—

'Jilly?' Rich Blake, Max decided, was as crass and stupid as he had expected him to be, but at the sound of his voice Jilly immediately stiffened in his arms, became self-conscious. The moment was over and he let her go, turned to Blake. He was standing a few steps below them, staring up at Jilly. 'It is you. Petra said it couldn't be, but I was sure...' He glanced at Max, frowning, then turned back to her. 'You didn't say you were coming here.'

'Jilly didn't know,' Max intervened smoothly, forcing Blake to look at him while she recovered her poise. 'It was a surprise.'

Rich Blake laughed. 'It surprised the hell out of me, I can tell you. I didn't know you were part of the night-club crowd.' He looked at Jilly, then more pointedly at Max, demanding an introduction.

'Oh, sorry, Richie. Max, may I introduce Rich Blake? You may have heard of him.' She flickered a glance at Max and he felt a quick glow of pleasure at the ease with which she had caught on, at the way they had become fellow conspirators.

'I think maybe I have,' he said. And he held out his hand.

'Richie, this is Max Fleming.'

'Max.' Richie took Max's hand and waited for some further explanation. Then, when it wasn't forthcoming, he dropped it. 'Why don't you come over and join us?'

'Not tonight, Richie,' Jilly said, before Max could intervene. 'It's been a long day.'

'Maybe another time,' Max added, and using his good leg and the bannister rail rose, with some difficulty, to his feet. Jilly stood up with him and put her arm about his waist, her shoulder beneath his arm, offering a discreet prop should he need it. Then he said, 'I think someone's looking for you, Blake.'

Rich turned. 'Oh, Petra. I was just coming.' He turned back to Jilly. 'Someone wants to take photographs for a magazine. Better do it before things get too wild.'

Jilly gave Petra a little wave, then looked up at Max, a question in her eyes. He gave a slight nod. 'Bye, Richie,' she said.

'I'll call you tomorrow, Jilly.'

But she was already walking up the stairs. 'Lean on me, Max,' she murmured.

'I'm sorry about this—'

'You warned me you were a crock. Next time don't be a vain one, bring your magic wand—you can use it as a walking stick.'

Next time. There shouldn't be a next time. Not if he had any sense. 'Thanks,' he said as they reached the street level. 'I think I can manage now.'

'You're sure?'

Her arm was still hooked about him, his arm was still around her shoulders, and from where he stood Max could see Rich Blake, eyes narrowed, still watching them.

Max smiled down at her. 'No point in taking any chances, I suppose,' he said, keeping his arm exactly where it was. But it took all his will-power not to kiss her again. 'Did you enjoy that?'

Jilly said nothing. She wasn't entirely sure what he was talking about. The nightclub, the dancing, the kiss. No one had ever kissed her like that before, as if her pleasure was the only thing that mattered, giving not taking.

'It's all right, Jilly, I won't tell.'

And then she realised he wasn't talking about any of those, but about Petra. 'Did you see her face?' Jilly pulled away, wrapping her arms about herself as she gave a little shiver. Petra had looked lost, uncertain. She had been the cause of that and she hated it. 'I know exactly how she was feeling. I was there myself a few hours ago.' She shook her head. 'No. There's no pleasure in hurting anyone.'

'Not even when she gunked you?'

'How did you know that was deliberate?'

He hadn't. 'You weren't going to be allowed to win, were you?' Then he said, 'Prince Charming is still there, watching us. Do you want to leave him a shoe?'

'Why?' Max was looking at her quizzically and she suddenly realised that he was joking. 'Oh, I see.' Then, with a sudden return to down-to-earth practicality, 'That would be the most terrible waste of a lovely pair of shoes.'

'You're going to make him work for it, then?'

At least she had no noticeable inclination to stay and dance until dawn with a man who had two legs in good working order. But Max congratulated himself too soon because she grinned and said, 'I don't think I would count on Richie to work very hard for anything, except work itself. If he wants to get in touch he has my phone number.'

'You know, Jilly, I don't believe your heart is entirely in this Cinderella thing,' he said.

She looked up at him for a moment. 'Actually, Max, I think I've lost the plot. I thought we were going to gatecrash Richie's party tonight, wow him with my glamour and then walk away.'

Walk away? She'd planned on walking away? 'Hardly gatecrash—you were invited, Jilly.'

'Yes, well…' She glanced down at her finery. 'I went to a heck of a lot of trouble for one glass of champagne and two dances.' And a kiss, she thought. And a kiss. It had been worth it just for the kiss.

'It was worth it,' he assured her, his words mirroring her thoughts. 'I told you he'd notice you.'

She considered suggesting reinforcing the message with another kiss. Then decided that it would be greedy. 'Mmm. Well, I'll get my coat and then you can run the plan by me again on the way home.'

'I didn't have a plan,' he said, helping her into the car a few minutes later. 'But I do now.'

'So?' she demanded.

'You're not going to like it.'

'Try me.'

He glanced at the driver. 'Let's leave it until we're home.'

Twenty minutes later she was sitting beside the fire in his study with a glass of brandy in her hand.

'So.' She lay her head back against the rubbed leather of the armchair. 'Tell me about your plan.'

'To keep you as far away from Rich Blake as possible.'

She sipped the brandy. 'I like it so far.'

'Do you?' So, sweet Jilly wanted to make Rich Blake suffer a little, did she? Well, that was just fine with him. 'Well, good, because I'm afraid that I'm being thoroughly selfish.' In his experience, people were quicker to accept a selfish motive than an altruistic one. 'You see, I need you and it occurs to me that once Blake realises what he's missing you'll be out of here faster than a squirrel up a tree and I won't have anyone to put up with my short temper and unsocial hours.'

'That's true.' And she came close to smiling. For a man who could kiss like that she would put up with a lot. 'But who said anything about leaving?'

'The minute Richie gets his hands on you he's going to want you all to himself.'

'Maybe he will...' then she couldn't meet his eyes any longer '...but I'm not a pushover, Max.'

'I didn't say you were. But I saw the way he was looking at you.' Stunned. He rolled the glass between his hands, warming it. 'You've known him a long time and you came to London to be near him. I don't imagine you were planning on living with your cousin for long.' He had been staring into his glass, now he looked up and confronted her. 'And you haven't been looking for anywhere of your own, have you?'

She swallowed some of the brandy. 'You said it, Max. With all those long hours, when have I had the time?'

'If you'd wanted time you would have asked for it.'

'I suppose so.' Her face was in shadows, but Max heard the doubt in her voice. What had she planned, then? She'd come racing down to London on the promise of a job just to be near the man... He stopped. She hadn't really thought it through, he realised. And then he frowned. He had assumed that Rich Blake had been her first lover, that bitter-sweet relationship that never truly left you, and that was why she had been so angry at his neglect. But suppose that wasn't the case?

She was curled up in the armchair opposite him, leaning back against the old leather, and she was all woman, every inch of her. Her full mouth, the swell of her breasts beneath the pale satin, the inviting flare of her hips as she had danced proclaimed her womanhood. But now, suddenly, doubt began to niggle at him. It was surely impossible, in this day and age, that she had never—

'Tell me about him,' he said quickly, rather than think the impossible. 'I want to understand the man.'

The house was so quiet that all Jilly could hear was her own ragged breath, the almost painful beat of her pulse hammering against her ears. She stared at the amber liquid pooled in the bottom of her glass and wondered what on earth she was doing, sitting, late at night, with nothing but the glow of the fire to illuminate them, talking about Richie to a man she scarcely knew, a man who had kissed her so that her body soared, promising almost unimaginable pleasures.

She glanced at him stretched out in his armchair on the other side of the hearth, staring into the tiny flickers of flame. He'd thrown his jacket over a chair in the corner, loosened his tie, undone the top stud fastening his collar.

A thick wedge of hair had fallen forward over his forehead but he didn't push it back with the impatient flick of his hand as he did when he was working. Instead he left it to lie at peace where it fell.

The red glow from the fire threw his face into sharp relief, dark shadows hiding his eyes while the firelight burnished his sharp cheek-bones, a long, thin nose, heating lips set in a hard line as if it was his habit to suppress what he was feeling.

That thought almost made her smile. He felt no need to suppress his feelings when it came to finding fault, yet despite his sister's warning, despite his own admission that he was impossibly demanding, with an irritation-point scarcely above zero, she enjoyed working for him, although it was easy to see why some people might find him difficult.

He was just so quick that if you lost concentration for even a minute you would never catch up again. But his passion for the work he was doing was infectious, his impatience with the slow workings of bureaucracy when children were dying admirable, if not always comfortable to work with.

Oh, come on, Jilly! Her subconscious gave her a little jab. This isn't anything to do with how he is to work with, the good job he's doing for starving children. This is about the way his hands felt as he held you, about the way he kissed you. Until then you'd have waltzed off in Richie's arms without a backward glance. Suddenly, she realised with a shock, Richie was about as interesting as yesterday's newspaper. A leftover relationship from adolescence that had never been resolved.

If he'd done what any other young man in his situation would have done, she would have got him out of her system long ago. But while she had been sitting at home working out how to make him a star, he had been pursuing other girls, Gemma even... The truth was that the chemistry just hadn't been there for them, never would be. She hadn't understood that until she had come face to face with the real thing.

What would Max do, she wondered, if she crossed the room, slid onto his lap, wrapped her arms about his neck and kissed him? Her body burned at the thought and she took another incautious gulp of the brandy. For a split second she came close to gagging as the fiery heat slid over her tongue. Max was out of his chair and across the room in a second, his broad hand thumping her back. She coughed, then threw out her arm to stop him.

'Are you all right?' Max asked, looking down at her. His hand remained against her spine, his thumb moving in a gentle caressing motion against her shoulder blades. All right? Had he no idea what he was doing to her? Or was he still so lost in his dead wife's memory that he was utterly incapable of noticing?

'Fine,' she said, a little hoarsely. Cleared her throat. 'Fine, really.' If he wasn't touching her like a lover, she didn't want him to touch her at all. And she leaned forward, easing away from his touch with the pretence of taking another sip of the brandy. 'See?'

He hesitated for a moment and then returned to his own chair. 'Why don't you tell me about him?' he said after a moment.

If talking about Richie kept her in this still, quiet space with Max, she would talk all night. So she concentrated on Richie, remembering that first morning when she had seen him cowering against the wall in the school yard, his glasses knocked sideways as he'd thrown up his arm to wipe the tears away on his sleeve.

'I was eight, I suppose, when I first saw him,' she began. 'He was older, nine, rising ten, but he was a year behind and so small for his age that I didn't realise. He never did grow very big.' Tonight in that ridiculously bright jacket he had looked even smaller than she remembered. Smaller than Max. She took another sip of the brandy. 'He was standing in the school playground, a pathetic scrap of a thing with hair so pale that he looked bald and a pair of spectacles stuck together with insulating tape and it hadn't taken two minutes for the bully boys to scent new prey.'

'So you pitched in and rescued him?'

'Someone had to. I couldn't just ignore it.'

'Couldn't you?' Then Max shook his head, not needing an answer. In truth, it was all too easy to imagine her wading in, a bossy eight-year-old throwing her weight about, putting the world to rights with a few swift blows from her lunch-box. The kind of girl that terrified even the biggest bully boys. He recalled the way she had taken control of the situation after his knee had given way on the stairs of the nightclub. No missish hysterics. No embarrassment even when someone had suggested that he might be drunk. And he had taken shocking advantage of the situation. If Rich Blake hadn't interrupted—

'Unfortunately after that I was stuck with him,' Jilly said, dragging him away from the sweet recollection of that moment when her lips had made him forget all pain, giving a whole new meaning to 'kissing it better'.

'He knew a good thing when he saw it.'

Jilly stared at the drink in her hand. He'd told his audience that she had followed him about, but it had been the other way around. 'He followed me every-where, and believe me, he had a real knack for getting into trouble. It wasn't just the playground bullies. He had this way of irritating teachers, just driving them crazy, and he didn't even know he was doing it. He just lived in a little world all of his own.'

'Adults do tend to find that annoying.'

'They just couldn't see beyond the forgotten home-work, the mislaid books. I spent more time nagging him about doing his own homework than getting on with my own.'

'Shouldn't his mother have been doing that?'

'She left home when he was a baby, just abandoned him.' She swallowed another mouthful of brandy. 'His father wasn't exactly Dad of the Year material, either. We had that in common.' The spirit was making her feel warm and relaxed. And talkative. Max glanced at her sharply when she mentioned her father, but she didn't want to talk about him. 'All Richie ever cared about was music,' she went on. 'Pop music,' she added, in case he was in any doubt. 'At school they thought he was lazy, but he wasn't, he'd do anything to earn money for equip-ment for his disco and he'd spend hours writing his links. He was brilliant at it, too. Different, you know? And he knew every record that had ever been pressed. There was nothing wrong with his mind except that it just ran on the one track. It should have been obvious to anyone who cared that he should be a DJ but, instead of helping him, at school they just tried to squeeze him into some little slot they had earmarked for no-hopers.'

'I think I read somewhere recently that Mick Jagger was told by his careers teacher to get a job in a building society.'

'It figures.' She sighed, took another little sip of brandy. 'I suppose they believe it's for the best. They just don't have any imagination.'

'Or too much. It could be they're imagining what life would be like as an out-of-work DJ.'

'Maybe.' She gave a little shrug. 'It is tough. Richie knew all there was to know about pop music but he hadn't the faintest idea how to sell himself.'

'He seems to have managed pretty well. He's the main man on one of the country's most successful commercial stations. And now he's broken through into television there'll be no stopping him. He's got the common touch.' Max picked up the decanter from the table beside him, leaned across and topped up her glass. 'How did he get his start?'

'My mum was on the PTA committee, organising the Christmas dance at school and at her wits' end with everything. I got my brother to print up some impressive leaflets for Richie's disco outfit on his computer and left one where she would find it.'

'Oh, that was sneaky.'

She laughed. 'The Head was livid, and so was my mother when she realised what I'd done. She thought she'd booked some professional outfit at a bargain price, but by the time they found out it was too late to do anything about it. He got some terrific publicity out of that.'

'Oh? And how did you manage that?'

'Me?'

'Don't tell me it wasn't your doing, Jilly,' he said, in that easy drawl. 'I'd be really disappointed.'

She shrugged. 'It wasn't difficult. I rang up the local paper, they're always desperate for that kind of ''human interest'' story. ''Schoolboy DJ Rocks the PTA.'' The trouble is not too many people want a fifteen-year-old DJ, no matter how good he is.' She grinned as she remembered. 'He could hardly see over the top of his sound-board.'

It occurred to Max that Jilly had earned Richie's friendship. She'd certainly earned better than a public dousing in gunge and a brush-off organised by a self-serving PA. 'I'm sure you didn't let that slow you down,' he said. 'What else did you do?'

'I made tapes of him rehearsing and sent them to the local radio station.'

'Good move.'

'It took a while. I think they saw him in the end just to stop me bombarding them with recordings. Of course once they'd seen him in action they gave him a slot, just fifteen minutes on a youth programme on Saturday mornings, but it was a start.'

'And then?'

She regarded him across the hearth. The firelight was burnishing his cheeks, the fine line of his mouth. Just looking at his mouth brought back the way he had kissed her like a blow to the midriff. 'And then…' For a moment she had completely forgotten what they were talking about. 'Oh, and then I recorded those and started sending them to the London commercial stations.'

'Have you ever considered a career in public relations?' He didn't wait for an answer. 'How long did it take?' he asked.

'A couple of years, I suppose.'

'And then he moved to London and forgot all about you,' he said as a wave of hot jealousy made him cruel, made him long to jolt her out of the cosy glow of reminiscence and remember what had happened that evening.

CHAPTER SEVEN

JILLY was out of the chair like a rocket. 'That's not fair!' she said. Then realised how ridiculous she was to be so defensive of Richie Blake. It was just that remembering how it had been, how she had looked after him, mothered him, had brought it all back.

'Isn't it?' He stared up at her. 'After what you've done for him I'd say that sending "I'm busy" messages via his secretary wasn't fair. I'd say that what happened this evening wasn't fair—'

'But that was Petra—'

'He owes you enough to make sure no one could do that to you. He should have cared enough—' He stopped himself. That was something she had to work out for herself, but his raw anger at the way she had been treated shocked him.

'He doesn't owe me anything, Max.' Then she shrugged. 'Except perhaps for all those tapes, all that postage.' She paused. 'Oh, and of course the rail fare to London.'

She could make a joke out of it? 'Of course. So do we send him a great big bill for your PR services, or shall we really give him something to think about?'

'What I did for him was out of genuine belief in his ability. Because I wanted to help.'

'Because you were in love with him?' She didn't answer and he reached for the decanter. 'Life's a bitch, Jilly.' He refilled his own glass and, after a moment's hesitation, refilled hers too. She was right, of course,

Blake owed her nothing. She had done all that for him because she had wanted to, because she had seen something special in him. And she had been right—perhaps that would be her only reward because life wasn't fair and love certainly wasn't fair. 'Life's a bitch,' he repeated, 'and then you die. Or maybe you don't. And sometimes that's worse. I know all about love and the fairness of things, you see. I know all about being left behind.' She glanced at him. 'I loved Charlotte to the point of obsession. Have you ever felt like that? Had to have something so badly that you're convinced that your life will never be worth living without it?' Jilly would have liked to have been able to shake her head, say no. But she was afraid that it was no longer true. 'I couldn't believe that she didn't love me, couldn't love me.'

'But she married you—'

'I pursued her with such single-mindedness, was convinced that if she married me I could make her love me. When she came to me and told me that her father had lost everything in the Lloyds crash, that she would marry me if I would bail him out—'

'Are you *that* rich?'

'Unfortunately, yes.' Then he lifted his shoulders. 'But shopping is no substitute for a life and when she met someone she really loved she could no longer bear to touch me.'

'She had an affair?' Jilly's voice betrayed her shock, her eyes huge and dark in the firelight.

Max had no idea how he had come to such revelations. Maybe because it was so long since he had talked to anyone like this. Maybe in the darkness he hadn't felt so exposed. But he couldn't leave Jilly believing that his wife had betrayed him.

'No. That would have helped, perhaps. I could have

blamed her for that. But my wife and my best friend were above that. It was heartbreaking to see them in the same room together, not looking at one another, not touching. Just hurting.'

'So why didn't you let her go?'

The accusation was there in her voice. 'Did you think I wouldn't?' If only it had been that easy. 'Dominic was a devout Catholic, Jilly. He could never have married a divorced woman and anything else would never have been enough.'

Jilly sank to her knees in front of the fire, staring up at him. 'Is that why they died? Together?'

She was quick to see the possibilities, but she was wrong. 'No, it was an accident, Jilly. I was the one who was supposed to die.' He heard the sharp intake of breath. 'There was nothing else I could do for her.' He stared for a long time into the bottom of his glass. 'She loved to ski and I thought perhaps the chance to get out on the mountains would help take her mind off things. I took her to a small village in the Alps, miles from anywhere. Someone must have told him, maybe she told him—he couldn't stay away.' He had understood that. 'He was the first person we saw as we walked through the door of the village inn. It was as if I was getting a message, that this was the place to bow out...'

'Oh, Max!'

'It was a perfect morning, still, clear. It had snowed in the night and it lay on everything like icing on a wedding cake. A beautiful day to die.' Jilly's muffled cry brought him back from that perfect moment when everything had seemed like that morning—crystal clear and bright. 'Something must have woken her or maybe she wasn't asleep at all.' He glanced at Jilly. 'She must have realised what was in my mind because she woke

Dom and they came after me. I heard them shouting, calling my name. I was heading for the edge when they saw me. They tried to cut across my path and then…and then…' He paused as the scene came back to haunt him, as it had done every day of his life since. 'The fresh snow began to slip and I was swept off my feet and then everything went black.' He shivered, as if remembering the cold. He had been cold ever since, deep down inside.

'Max—' She put her hand on his, dragging him back to the present. He stared at it, small, white, warm against his skin. 'I think that's the saddest thing I've ever heard. Such a waste.'

'Yes, a terrible waste of two fine people.'

For a long moment they seemed to be locked together in the same place, a place where the touch of her hand was something more than skin against skin. Then, very carefully, she took her hand away and turned to stare into the fire.

'I shouldn't have told you. I don't know why I did.'

'You didn't want me feeling sorry for myself.'

'And I don't want you feeling sorry for me, either. I was selfish, thinking of myself when I married her. If I'd loved her enough I would have bailed out her father and walked away.'

'She didn't have to do it, Max.'

'She loved her family. She did it for them. I did it for myself.' He picked up the decanter. 'Have a drop more of this,' he said with determined brightness, topping up her empty glass, 'and I'll tell you my plan.'

Empty? When had she drunk all that?

Jilly shrugged and folded herself up on the floor at his feet, leaning back against the arm of his chair, sipping the lovely warming liquid, wanting to go to him, hold him. But he would misunderstand. She wasn't entirely sure she understood herself. 'I'm listening,' she said.

'It's nothing complicated. I just thought that you might enjoy making young Mr Blake chase you for a change.'

She turned to look up at him. 'Chase me? Why would he do that when he's got women chasing him?'

'You think he won't bother?'

'I know he won't.'

Max lifted his brows the barest fraction.

'Why should he?'

'Curiosity, perhaps. A little niggle of doubt that he might have let something special slip through his fingers.'

She turned away, shaking her head.

'Simple lust, then,' he offered and she gave a hoot of derisory laughter. It didn't fool him for a minute. 'What's the matter, Jilly? Scared he won't be interested?' Then, 'Or scared that he will?'

'No!' Then, 'It's just—'

'What?' He leaned forward, hooked his fingers beneath her chin, forcing her to turn and look up at him, needing to see her eyes.

'I know you're trying to be kind, Max, but it's the brandy talking. I can't possibly compete with the kind of women Richie had in tow tonight.' In truth, she had no wish to compete; tonight the scales had fallen from her eyes. Richie was a user, a taker and she had given more than enough. If he had thought anything of her, he would have been in touch a long time ago, eager to share his success. If he wanted her now, because she suddenly looked good, it meant nothing.

In the firelight Jilly's eyes were dark, unreadable. She was worth ten of any of the women that flocked around men like Rich Blake, Max knew; she was fresh and lovely and good and kind. But when it came right down to it she was just a nice girl dressed up for a night out. She would need polish, style, to survive in the jungle inhabited by the Rich Blakes of this world. Well, he could do that for her. It would be little enough in return for the kiss he had stolen. 'Give me a week,' he said, 'and I'll make you the most talked about woman in London.'

'A whole week? It would take that long?' As if she cared. There was only one man she wanted to notice her and he seemed determined to pass her on as quickly as possible...just as long as it didn't interfere with his work schedule.

'Don't be sarcastic, Jilly. It isn't ladylike.'

'I'm enough of a lady to know that being talked about isn't ladylike either,' she replied.

He eased his shoulders into a long, thoughtful shrug. 'Maybe not—it rather depends what is being said. But it would give that cousin of yours something to think about when she comes back from Florida. And it would seriously irritate Petra.'

'That's true and it's a nice idea, Max, but I really don't think Richie will be ringing me again and, frankly, irritating Petra isn't particularly high on my list of things to do in London.'

'Regretting not leaving that shoe after all?' he asked. Max didn't know why he was persisting with this. Maybe it had been that particularly nasty bout of self-pity that had attacked him earlier in the evening; this was a chance to stop feeling sorry for himself, do something for someone else. To do something utterly unselfish.

Or maybe it was because ever since Jilly had moved

into his house he kept having odd thoughts, sudden long-ings, echoes in his head of the man he had once been.

Or maybe he just liked the idea of showing her a good time. The fact that she was thinking about another man when she was dancing with him would be sufficiently chilling to keep any ridiculous ideas he might have about her firmly under control.

'You know that he'll be curious about me, Jilly. He'll want to know who I am, how you met me. He'll be curious about what you're doing in London. You sur-prised him tonight; he won't be able to stop himself thinking about you. And of course there's tomorrow.' She still looked doubtful. 'You'll be in the newspaper. There'll be a lot of interest in you and we'll stoke it up tomorrow. Where would you like to go?'

'Tomorrow? You can't really mean you want to do this again?' Could he? She stood up. Too quickly. The room spun as the brandy went straight to her legs. Max was beside her in an instant to steady her. 'Oops,' she said, leaning against him. Then she giggled.

With his arms about her, Max came to the conclusion that Rich Blake needed his head testing as well as his eyes. But the man was new to success and it was easy to see how the sparkle might have blinded him to the gold right beneath his nose. 'I thought you were a fighter, Jilly. Are you really going to stand back and let those half-naked hussies get away with the man you helped to make into a success?'

'They're welcome to him.'

'You don't mean that.'

Actually, she did. She might have had too much brandy but she knew that. But something stopped her from saying it. It was to do with the way that Max was holding her. The memory of dancing in his arms. The blissful memory of the way he had kissed her. If she pretended, he might just kiss her again… It would be worth it, even if it was just to make Richie jealous.

'I can't compete with some woman wearing nothing but fishnet and half a dozen sequins,' she said, sidetracking a declaration of the truth. 'I'm not built for a dress that exposes that much flesh.'

Max could have disputed that, but didn't. 'It's not what she shows that makes a woman desirable, Jilly. Real men like to unwrap their own presents.' She blushed; even in the red glow of the firelight the sudden flush to her cheeks was unmistakable. The innocence was genuine, no doubt about it. Maybe Harriet was right, maybe it would be wiser to put her on the first available train to Newcastle. But the wisdom sector of his brain seemed to be having a day off because he said, 'If you really love him, you owe it to yourself to make a stand.'

'Like Custer?' And she giggled again. He cursed himself for a fool and removed the glass from her hand before she could drink any more.

'Exactly like Custer. All or nothing.' She might be safer going home and finding some ordinary man to love, but if she did there would always be a part of her wondering… It would eat at her. Undermine any future relationship with a hundred 'What if?'s. Her only chance was to see enough of Rich Blake to realise that she was chasing after someone who no longer existed. Rich Blake might use her, as he was undoubtedly using Petra and any other girl who caught his eye, but it was unlikely that he would marry her—something Max was certain the red-headed assistant had already found out the hard way.

It was that thought that made it possible for him to stand back, his hands on her shoulders, look her in the eye and say with all sincerity, 'I promise you, Jilly, whatever happens you can't lose.'

'Honest?' She looked at him with eyes that would have melted an iceberg and he felt like an utter heel, because what he meant and she understood by the words 'can't lose' were a world apart.

'Honest,' he replied, and with his finger he drew a cross over her heart, the way she had done that first morning. It was a mistake. Beneath the satin he felt her body respond to his touch. His own skin tightened dangerously, began to ache with longing. But she was looking at him, expecting an answer to something she had said. 'What?'

'How are we going to do it?' she repeated.

We. The word gave him an odd little charge of excitement. It was a long time since he had been part of that particular combination. With that 'we' all doubts were cast aside.

'Easy. We'll join the party people, go to a few fancy restaurants, dance the night away at the clubs and you'll get your picture in the papers. You'll be noticed.'

'Noticed?' Her eyes were alight at the thought. 'Who by?'

'Everyone. But Rich Blake mostly, although I think we'll try and avoid him for a little while. Let's see if we can persuade him to come looking for you.' Not that he had any doubt. She looked fabulous tonight, but once she had been through the polisher the man wouldn't be able to help himself. What man would? 'It'll be a new experience for him.'

'Why, Max?' He looked down into a pair of soft brown eyes that flickered with the golden reflected firelight. 'Why are you doing this? And don't tell me it's just because I'm the best shorthand-typist in London and you're not prepared to lose me, because I won't believe you.'

'All right, I'll level with you.' She waited, her lips slightly parted in expectation of some great revelation. Instead he said, 'Amanda thinks I should get out more.'

If he had hit her she couldn't have looked more shocked. 'Your sister?'

'She keeps telling me that I work too hard, don't get out enough, that I look like... Well, you get the picture. If I'm seen around town with you she'll stop worrying for a while.' Then he shrugged. 'And dancing is a lot more fun than working out in that damned gym.'

For a moment she had believed him. 'Horse feathers,' she said, as an advance on pig's eyes.

'It's true, I promise,' he said, suddenly solemn.

'I didn't mean about the dancing, I meant...' Her voice trailed off. 'You know what I meant.'

'Does it matter, Jilly? You saw the look on Petra's face tonight when she realised the kind of competition she's got? Won't it be worth it just to see Blake's reaction when he realises that little Jilly Prescott is no longer waiting to leap to attention whenever he snaps his fingers, to be there when he needs someone to fill in at the last minute? That if he wants your attention in future he's going to have to work for it?'

No. She wasn't interested. And yet...

Max saw the beginning of a smile deepen the corners of her mouth as the wicked idea slithered into her mind and lodged there as he had known it would. It started small and grew, until her lips parted and the smile broke into a chuckle of laughter.

'You're bad, Max,' she said, giggling helplessly and leaning against him, her cheek against his shirt front.

Innocent was right. 'You're appealing to my very worst instincts.'

'If that's what it takes,' he admitted, his voice suddenly thick as his arm found its way about her shoulders. 'But are your worst instincts listening?'

Jilly giggled again and as she looked up at him Max acknowledged that she had been right about one thing. He was feeling very bad indeed.

Why on earth had he ever thought her mouth too large? It was generous, warm, inviting. Her face was not conventionally pretty, but it was strong and it could be beautiful in the way that the French had of being beautiful that had nothing to do with that English peaches-and-cream prettiness, everything to do with drama, profile.

He pushed the unruly mop of hair back from her face. It was all he could do to resist the impulse to rake his fingers through it, twist it in his fingers before lowering his mouth to hers and doing his level best to make her forget that Blake existed. Selfish. The word hammered at him. 'The first thing we must do is get this cut,' he said, with difficulty, as the sudden, unlooked-for ache in his groin caught him by surprise. Carefully he let her hair fall, his arm drop, and he stepped back. He was doing this for her, not for himself. Jilly didn't want to forget Rich Blake.

'Cut?' She snapped out of the warm brandy-and-champagne-induced euphoria. 'Are you kidding? My mother would have a fit if I had it cut—'

'You're a big girl now, Jilly, and this…' he fanned out a handful of hair before letting it drop '…lacks the sophistication you're going to need. Tomorrow you can go through the wardrobe upstairs and pick out whatever dresses you like. Then I'll take you to dinner at the kind of restaurant where celebrities go to be seen, followed by a visit to a nightclub. Just to make sure.'

'Sure?'

'That you're talked about, sure that Rich Blake hears.'

Her dark brows drew together as she considered this. 'How will he know it's me?'

'How many Jilly Prescotts are there?'

Jilly swallowed hard. Maybe it was the brandy, or maybe the warmth of the fire, but she felt light-headed. Not herself at all, but quite beautiful suddenly. It was the way Max was looking at her. The way he always looked at her, as if he could see more than everyone else.

'I don't know, Max… I'm not sure…'

He brushed away her objections. 'Give it a try to-morrow, Jilly. If you don't enjoy yourself then we'll forget it and all I ask in return is that you stay until Laura gets back. Is it a deal?' Every instinct was telling him that the only way to seal this kind of bargain was with a kiss. He resisted. His brain might be out to lunch but it would be back and then it would give him hell. So he held out his hand and, after a last moment of hesitation, she took it.

'It's a deal, Max.'

'I think we should drink to that.' He gave her back her glass—it had little more than a sip left in it—and touched it with his own. 'To your heart's desire.'

She looked at him for a long moment and then raised the glass, swallowed the remaining brandy. 'Thank you, Max.'

'No need to thank me, Jilly. Whatever happens I still have you as a secretary, so I win.'

'And me?'

He found it hard to meet her direct gaze. 'I told you, Jilly, you can't lose.'

The ringing of the telephone woke her. Jilly moaned and turned over, ignoring it. It continued to ring. She covered her head with a pillow. Still it rang. Desperate to stop a noise that was going through her like a dentist's drill, she eased herself out of bed and, with a hand to her head to catch it in the very likely event that it fell off, she slowly covered the distance to the infernal machine. Then she lifted the receiver, dropped it on the floor and staggered back to bed.

She had no sooner closed her eyes than a hammering began at the door. She couldn't believe it. What was so urgent? Anyone would think World War Three had broken out while she was asleep. And if it had there was nothing she could do about it. But she dragged herself to the door, opened it.

Max didn't wait for an invitation, he walked straight past her and into the kitchen where he put the kettle on. Then he unwrapped two fizzy hangover cure tablets and dropped them into a small glass of water. 'Plink, plink, fizz,' he said, passing it to her.

She said something unprintable in return but took the glass, swallowed her medicine and then shuddered, hugely.

'You're not used to brandy?' he suggested.

The very word made her want to throw up. 'I recall two or three glasses of champagne as well,' she whispered pointedly. 'I'm not used to alcohol of any description in that quantity.'

'I should have realised, sorry. *I* won't let it happen again.'

'You won't be consulted, Max. I won't let it happen again.'

'Right.' He glanced at her. Today the T-shirt didn't have the saving grace of even an open dressing gown to lend it a modicum of decency but there wasn't a repeat of the scramble for modesty. She didn't seem to have noticed, while he was noticing too much. 'Go and get dressed, Jilly,' he said. 'We've a lot to get through this morning. I'll make you some coffee and toast.'

'I don't want anything. I just want to go back to sleep for the rest of the weekend. Shut the door as you leave.'

'Two glasses of brandy and you're finished?'

'For an economist, Max, your reckoning leaves a lot to be desired,' she said, wincing as she put her hand to her head. 'And if you're feeling no pain this morning I'd say you've got a problem.'

'The only problem I've got is you. I've sold my soul for an appointment with a hairdresser who is usually booked three months in advance.'

'Your soul?'

'Okay, I exaggerated. Four tickets to the opening night of the next Lloyd Webber musical.'

'How did you get them?' She held up a hand. 'No, don't tell me. Your soul. You were overcharged.'

'That's debatable, but even so I can assure you that going back to bed is not an option.'

Jilly looked at him mutinously from beneath a mane of hair that looked as if it hadn't been near a hairdresser in three years, let alone three months. 'Suppose I don't want my hair cut?'

'Jilly, if you haven't showered and dressed in ten minutes I will cut your hair myself,' he warned. 'With a pair of garden shears.'

She stared at him. 'Geez, don't you get out of bed crabbity?'

'While you're a little ray of sunshine, I suppose? Let me tell you that I've been up since six-thirty. If you'd done the same and gone for your usual run this morning, you wouldn't be feeling so rough.'

'I wouldn't be feeling anything. I'd be dead,' she countered, but cheered considerably at the possibility that he was feeling more like she was than he was prepared to admit.

'Now who's exaggerating?'

'All right,' she said, surrendering without further argument because it was obvious he was not going to go away—a fact that left her feeling a lot more cheerful than it should have done. 'Make it orange juice and forget the toast and I'll be right with you.'

The shower helped, along with a large dollop of moisturiser to deal with the dehydration. She dressed without much thought in jeans and a long-tailed shirt. Then she added a waistcoat and looped a long printed chiffon scarf a couple of times around her neck. She screwed up her eyes to stare at her reflection in the mirror and decided that it was just as well that she couldn't see up close too well without her glasses.

'Here.' Max put a tall glass of freshly squeezed orange juice into her hand a moment later when she walked through to the kitchen. Her hand, she was pleased to note, didn't actually shake as she gratefully sipped the juice.

'I think I'll stick to this in future,' she said.

'Famous last words.'

'Possibly, but whatever you do don't give me brandy again, Max. Ever.'

'Not even if you faint?'

'I make it a rule never to faint.' She made it a rule never to drink too much either, a hollow little voice reminded her. Hedging her bets, she added, 'However, in the unlikely event that I do, just throw water. It's quicker, cheaper and less painful.'

'I'll remember that,' Max said, and grinned. Grinned? Max Fleming was grinning? It was almost worth the hangover to see those laughter lines about his eyes used to proper effect. 'Are you ready to go?'

She put the glass down on the worktop, her hand suddenly all over the place. 'You're sure about this, Max? I know you're trying to be kind—'

'And you could try the patience of a saint. We went through all your objections last night.'

'But—'

'We don't have time for this, Jilly. We can't keep the man with the scissors waiting.'

'Well, I don't suppose a haircut will kill me.' Grievous bodily harm she wasn't so sure about. She hated going to the hairdresser's, but comforted herself with the thought that someone with a three-month waiting list was unlikely to make a total mess of the job.

And it would give her time to think of some way out of his ridiculous scheme to make her playmate of the month because, in the cold, sober light of a January morning, it was obvious she couldn't possibly go through with it.

'What on earth are we going to do with this?'

'I'd just like a trim,' Jilly said firmly.

Max had accompanied her to the hairdresser's in the chauffeur-driven limousine that had been waiting for them at the gate but, once there, he'd abandoned her to the less-than-tender mercies of a diminutive, black-clad

Cockney whose fingers appeared to be welded to a pair of dagger-sharp scissors.

The man with the scissors ignored her reply, walking slowly around her twice before lifting his eyes to the ceiling and muttering something that might have included the word 'haystack' although she doubted whether he had ever seen one outside a colouring book.

It was obvious from this reaction that his question had been rhetorical, that any further suggestion she might offer would only bring further scorn down upon her poor aching head. She was right. After summoning one of his assistants, he spun round and walked off.

Assuming from this that her hair was beneath his contempt, that she had been given a reprieve, Jilly was about to head for the door and tell Max that he could keep his precious tickets when a girl appeared at her side determined upon swathing her in a vast white gown. Smiling sympathetically, which Jilly did not consider a good sign, she draped the gown about Jilly's shoulders and led her out of sight where presumably she wouldn't frighten the other clients. 'Take a seat at the basin, will you?' the girl said. 'And I'll wash your hair.'

Well, that didn't sound too dangerous, and the slow, careful massaging of her scalp was bliss, lulling Jilly into a false sense of security because after that everything happened very fast. That was when she realised she should have been a great deal firmer when the maestro with the scissors had asked that first question, rhetorical or not.

There was a long, still moment while he regarded her, eyes narrowed intently, through the mirror. Then there was a whirl of scissors as her crowning glory, the result of years of nurturing, careful trimming of split ends and hot-oil conditioning, was attacked without mercy. For one horrified moment she stared as it fell away in vast chunks and then, because by then it was too late to shout 'Stop!', she slammed her eyes shut and wished she'd called Max's bluff about the garden shears. Even if he had meant it, the result couldn't have been more drastic and it would have been a heck of a lot cheaper.

After what seemed like a lifetime, the demon barber stopped. Stopped, turned on his heel and walked away without a word.

She peered at her reflection. It was worse than anything she could have imagined. Her hair, or most of it, lay in heaps about her on the floor. All that remained were a few damp tendrils clinging to her scalp and her cheeks.

After that she didn't care what happened. Someone else led her away and did nightmarish things with silver foil, and she contented herself with the cold comfort that there was no longer any question of her eating in some glamorous and expensive nosherie with Max Fleming. He'd take one look and run a mile.

Then it was washed again and conditioned and blow-dried. And finally the madman with the scissors reappeared, all smiles now as he took his instrument of torture for another ride over what remained of her hair while she flinched, eyes closed, not wanting to see what he had done. Then there was a pause. A hush of expectancy.

His assistant touched her shoulder. 'You can look now,' she said. Jilly didn't want to look but, unable to put off the moment of truth any longer, she slowly opened her eyes. Then she blinked. That wasn't her. That girl with the delicate froth of sun-streaked hair couldn't be her. Could it? She lifted her hand to touch her hair and the reflection mirrored her action.

She swallowed, glanced at the black-clad figure waiting for her to say something. 'It's different,' she said. He made no response. 'I can't ever remember having short hair. My mother will...' Have a fit. Her mother would quite definitely have a fit. Quite suddenly she didn't care what her mother thought. 'You've done something to the colour,' she said.

The man with the three-month waiting list shrugged. 'Just put in a little sunshine.'

Sunshine. Yes, that was it exactly. Her dark hair now looked as if the sun were shining through it. 'Thank you,' she said. The words seemed inadequate but they were apparently enough because he simply nodded and moved on to the woman in next chair who kept him waiting while she leaned across to Jilly and touched her hand.

'I saw you arrive,' she said. 'I can't believe you're the same girl.'

Continuing to stare at her reflection, Jilly said, 'Actually, I don't think I am.' Then she turned and realised that her neighbour was a woman she watched regularly on the television.

Well, so what? She had been on television too. It was no big deal.

The girl who handed her her coat informed her that her car was waiting and she left the salon feeling thoroughly light-headed and eager to see what impression her new hairdo would make on Max.

Max had seen her coming, had a moment in which to come to terms with the transformation. He had always recognised she was more than the girl hiding behind a tiresome mop of hair but even he found it difficult to believe that she could be this woman, with the kind of face that, now it had been given a chance to shine, would make men stop in their tracks, turn and stare. It had happened as she'd crossed the pavement.

He climbed from the car, regarded her shorn locks for a moment, then said, 'Maybe I should have used the garden shears after all.'

For a moment she believed him, but only for a moment, then he saw a flicker of amusement in the depths of those large brown eyes—eyes that looked twice the size now they had no competition. It was the kind of amusement that only a woman supremely confident in the way she looked could manage. 'All complaints to the demon barber, Max. I wasn't given a choice in the matter.' And she stepped into the back of the limousine as if she had been born to it. 'So, what next?' she said, as he joined her and the driver closed the door behind him.

'Next we're going to buy you some shoes.'

'Shoes?'

'Charlotte's are too small and you'll never look beautiful if your feet hurt.'

He had intended to indulge himself by spoiling her, but it wasn't quite as easy as that. 'One pair is all I need,' she protested, when they had sorted out half a dozen pairs of evening shoes. 'One pair is all that I can afford. These silver ones are perfect, just like Charlotte's only they fit properly, and they'll go with just about anything.'

'I agree,' he said. It was simpler than getting into a haggle in the boutique. And while she was occupied paying for the silver sandals, he handed a credit card to the salesman and had the other five pairs taken to the car. 'If you'll excuse me, Jilly,' he said when she returned with an elegant black carrier, 'I've got a few things to do but the driver knows where to take you.'

'Oh? And where's that?'

'A health club. Facial, massage, whatever you want. It's all organised.'

She glanced at his cane. 'You keep the car, Max. I can easily take a taxi.'

No argument about the health club, he noted, only about transport. She was beginning to enjoy herself. Well, so was he. He lifted the cane to hail a passing cab. 'I've told Harriet to help you sort out the clothes. Take whatever you want because whatever is left is going to the charity shop on Monday.'

'Oh, but—'

'Be ready at eight-thirty. I've a table booked for dinner at nine.' Then he leaned forward and kissed her cheek. 'Did I tell you, you look absolutely gorgeous?'

He didn't wait for her reply and she was still standing on the pavement, her hand to her cheek, when his cab pulled away from the kerb.

CHAPTER EIGHT

ORGANISED was right. Jilly found herself pummelled and steamed and waxed and cleansed. Her nails were manicured and polished with a colour she chose from hundreds, a colour matched with a lipstick she bought for more than any lipstick had a right to cost.

Then she chose a sandwich from a menu the size of a house before having a lesson in make-up from a woman who seemed to be able to magic her perfectly ordinary bone structure into something that would look quite at home on the front cover of *Vogue*.

She floated back to the car and the driver's face said it all. 'Quite a transformation, miss.'

'From ugly duckling to swan in a day.'

'Hardly that, miss.'

'Oh?' Was she kidding herself after all?

The driver grinned. 'You weren't what I'd call an ugly duckling to start with.'

He'd been teasing. 'I think you'd better take me home, Bill. If I'm going to dance the night away, I'm going to need a little nap.'

But her phone was ringing when she arrived back at the flat, her mother wanting to talk about the television show. Wanting to complain about the way her daughter had been covered in gunge. 'What's the point of being a friend of the show's host,' she said, 'if he doesn't fix it so that you win?'

'That wouldn't have been fair, Mum,' she said patiently. But then nor was fixing it so that you lost. She was getting just a little tired of making excuses for Richie. Max had undoubtedly been right when he had said that Richie had only asked her to come to the show because someone had dropped out at the last moment.

But then if she had won, Max wouldn't have arrived to carry her away in his chauffeured limousine. Wouldn't have taken pity on her. Wouldn't have kissed her. She wondered how easy it would be to convince him that if he kissed her again, Richie might get really jealous.

She had only just hung up when Harriet rang. 'Are you coming over to sort out clothes, Jilly?'

She felt awkward about taking the clothes, but clearly Harriet had been briefed by Max, piling her up with far more than she would have been comfortable choosing for herself. 'I'm so glad he's decided to give these things away at last. It isn't healthy clinging onto the past, is it? Oh, this would suit you, Jilly!' She put a soft woollen dress on the pile to be carried across to the flat.

'I'm not too sure about this, Harriet. He won't want to see me wearing his wife's clothes.'

'Oh, good grief, child, you don't look a bit like Charlotte and she never wore anything more than two or three times.' Harriet shrugged. 'Unhappiness takes some women that way, but shopping is no substitute for love.' Harriet knew all about Charlotte and Max? 'Are you sure you won't take these furs?'

'What?' She stared at the glossy fur coats and jackets. 'Oh, quite sure.'

Harriet sighed. 'It's a pity. They cost the earth but I don't suppose the charity shop will want them either. I'll take them along to the Salvation Army, maybe they can find a use for them.'

'What was she like, Harriet? Mrs Fleming?'

'Charlotte?'

Jilly nodded.

'A golden girl. She had everything—beauty, wealth, a family tree that could be traced back to the Conquest.'

'But she wasn't happy.'

Harriet straightened from the pile of clothes she was sorting.

'Max told me what happened.'

'Did he? Told you how wonderful she was and how it was all his fault that she died?' She shook her head. 'She didn't have to marry him, Jilly. She just couldn't bear to let all that privilege go.' She loaded Jilly's arms with dresses. 'Couldn't bear to be without all this.'

'They must have cost a fortune.'

'She married him for his money. In the end all she could do was spend it. What are you going to wear tonight?'

Jilly glanced at the pile of dresses she was holding. 'I seem to be spoilt for choice.'

'You should try that black,' Harriet said, pointing at a dress that Jilly had discarded.

'I never wear black.' With her dark colouring she'd never felt right in it.

'Slip it on. Now that your hair has been brightened up you'll look good in it. And there's a black velvet evening coat somewhere—like the grey one you wore last night.'

Jilly's eyes widened. 'How did you know what I wore last night?' The coat and dress were in the flat.

Harriet grinned. 'Didn't you see your photograph in the *London News*? It's in the kitchen.'

'''Max Fleming and Jilly Prescott arriving at Spangles last night.''' Amanda Garland looked at the photograph of her brother—a man who had avoided anything remotely resembling a social occasion since the death of his wife—on the arm of a girl whom a few days ago she had worried might be too young, too plain, too gauche to be employed by her agency. It seemed she had been wrong and that Jilly Prescott had succeeded in catching her brother's eye when some of the loveliest girls in London had failed.

Amanda had seized the opportunity provided by Laura's prolonged absence to insinuate beautiful, eligible women right beneath her brother's nose, but he hadn't responded to any of them, except with irritation that they hadn't been able to match Laura's skills. Well, she hadn't exactly picked them for their secretarial abilities.

Yet this odd girl, with her northern bluntness, had managed to touch him. Maybe simply by needing him. She dropped the newspaper on the sofa table and with her voice in neutral said, 'Well, Max, I don't know what to say.'

'You don't have to say anything, Mandy. I just wanted to tell you myself before you saw the newspaper and jumped to all the wrong conclusions. And since someone is bound to phone Mother and tell her and she'll call you—'

'I get the picture.'

He shrugged.

'And there really is nothing to this apparent romance?' she persisted. 'It's simply to provoke Rich Blake into a fit of jealousy?'

'You did say I should get out more.'

Amanda didn't miss the evasion. 'Yes, I did, but I was almost certain you weren't listening.'

'Well, as you can see, I was.'

'Yes.' Amanda rubbed her hand over the sleeve of his jacket. 'It's just…you will be careful, darling?'

'Careful? Amanda, my dear, whatever can you be suggesting?'

If self-mockery was the order of the day she would play along with it and her smile matched his as she looked up at him. 'Only that if Rich Blake gets really jealous he might give you a black eye.'

'If it makes Jilly happy it will be worth it.'

'Really?' Did he realise what he was saying? Amanda's voice was diamond bright, even though her heart had plummeted at his words. 'I know she's a great shorthand-typist, Max, but I'd advise you not to take the knight errantry that far. A nightclub brawl would be so undignified.'

The black dress, a slender sheath of black silk chiffon, had needed nothing more than a tuck, provided by Harriet, to make it fit as if it had been made for her. Jilly, turning to check her reflection in an old cheval-mirror in the corner of her bedroom, remembered how it had felt when Max had put his arm around her waist and held her close to him, the imprint of his wife so vividly retained in his mind that he had known instantly that they were almost the same size. Almost. Charlotte had been a fraction taller, her waist a fraction larger.

Were the fractions enough, she wondered, or had it been Charlotte whom Max had been thinking of when he had held her close as they had danced at Spangles? Had it been the memory of his wife that had brought that dark, smoky look to his eyes just before he had kissed her? The thought brought a lump to Jilly's throat, a prickle of something suspiciously like tears to the back of her eyes that she didn't quite understand, or perhaps didn't want to understand.

She blinked, swallowed and concentrated very hard on fitting delicate spirals of silver to her ears, fastening the silver locket her mother had bought her for her eighteenth birthday about her neck. Then she stepped into the elegant high-heeled black shoes that Max had bought when her back had been turned, shoes that would have cost her two weeks' wages when she had been working at the firm of solicitors. Embroidered toes, elegant cross fastenings around the ankle, high, high heels. Oh, but they were beautiful.

Jilly turned again, faster this time so that the fluted hem of the dress swirled around her ankles. Maybe it was the unaccustomed colour, or her hair, or the sophisticated make-up, but she thought she looked older. Then she frowned—no, that wasn't it. What she looked was different. Grown up. Very grown up. She had never thought of herself as sexy. Buxom, perhaps, certainly far too big for the kind of clothes that skinny girls with their fashionable lack of a figure could wear. But the gown clung to her cleavage, emphasising curves that no longer looked *ample*, simply...tempting. Would Richie be tempted? Did she care? she wondered, pushing away the far more dangerous thought that seemed to have lodged itself at the back of her mind.

Then she smiled. Whatever Richie thought of the transformation, she decided, Petra would want to scratch her eyes out. Jilly might not begrudge her takeover of Richie, but she wasn't about to forget that deliberate dousing in gunge.

There was a tap at the door. 'Come in,' she called, and with one last twirl she picked up the black velvet coat and walked through to the living room. She had assumed it was Harriet, who had promised to come across and check that everything was exactly right, but it wasn't Harriet. It was Max. Tall, darkly compelling in his dinner jacket. She came to an abrupt halt in the doorway. 'I...I was just coming across to the house...'

Max felt his throat dry. There had been no time, no warning, no way to prepare himself for this stunning transformation. And Jilly Prescott had been transformed.

'A gentleman always calls for his date, Jilly.' Date? She was still thinking about that when he said, 'I'd better tell Amanda to start looking for another secretary on Monday.'

'I told you, Max, I'll stay until Laura comes back, whatever happens with Richie.'

She had told him, but he would never be able to work with her knowing that each evening she would be returning to the arms of another man. He took the velvet coat from her, held it so that she could slip her arms into the sleeves, so she had her back to him when he said, 'Rich Blake? I wasn't thinking about him. In fact, I'd say that if your Mr Blake isn't quick he's likely to be beaten in the crush.'

Jilly spun around. What did he mean by that? But Max was wearing an almost smile that gave nothing away. 'Oh, right,' she said. 'And that's your idea of a compliment, is it?'

'You want more?'

Everything. She wanted the whole nine yards. But she said, 'The suggestion that I'm likely to cause a stampede is some way short of the standard I would expect from a ''former playboy''. Maybe you're out of practice?'

Max swallowed hard. He had started this. He hadn't anticipated that it was going to be so difficult to stop.

But he shrugged, managed a smile. 'You think so? Well, maybe I am. Very well, let's see.'

He took a step back and, hand to chin, his eyes narrowed in concentration, he traversed her figure, starting at her toes and working slowly upwards.

Jilly, fervently wishing she had said nothing, waited, the heat rushing to her skin as he reached her 'tempting' cleavage. She made a move to fasten her coat; Max said nothing, simply raised an admonishing finger. Then, when he had completed his inspection, when the only sound was the clock ticking in the bedroom and her heart beating, he finally met her gaze. 'What would you like me to say, Jilly?'

'Nothing,' she said quickly, making a move to pick up her bag from the table. His eyes had said more than enough. They had told her that she was a stupid girl who didn't know when to keep her mouth shut.

'Your hair is quite lovely,' he said, reaching out to lift a tendril from her cheek, curling it about his finger, blocking her retreat. 'I can understand why the man has a waiting list.'

Jilly was very well aware that she had brought this upon herself and she had a finely tuned sense of when protest was pointless. 'I'll write him a note and tell him you approve. I'm sure he'll be delighted.'

Max tutted. 'Be gracious, Jilly. I'm doing my best. As you pointed out, I'm out of practice.'

Out of practice, my eye, Jilly thought. Then she stopped thinking and started to feel. She felt the cool touch of his hand against her cheek raising the soft down of her skin in an unexpected shiver of excitement, a shiver that spread through her body like lightning so that in seconds her entire skin seemed sensitised, on edge, waiting…

'Lovely skin, too,' he said, as if he hadn't been interrupted. And the backs of his fingers slid down her jaw, overloading her sensory system so that her insides threatened meltdown. Something was happening to her, something that she didn't entirely understand. Or maybe she did, but, because she knew that he was simply teasing her, she didn't want to understand. 'Thank you,' she said, a little hoarsely. Then, with a little move, 'Shouldn't we be going?'

'You've done something different with your make-up too.'

His hand was beneath her chin now, tilting her face so that she was forced to look up at him, meet him head on or close her eyes. Closing her eyes would be a dead give-away, but it was hard to look into those glittering grey eyes and keep pretending. If only she could tell what he was thinking, but he was still wearing that give-nothing-away expression, regarding her from beneath steeply lidded eyes, quizzical brows. Definitely teasing.

'Your eyes look twice the size. I hadn't noticed behind your glasses, behind all that hair, but they are a lovely colour. Golden…butterscotch…caramel…' He ran through the list, speaking more to himself than to her, discarding each of them in turn, clearly dissatisfied with the comparison. Then, 'Honey. Clear, dark honey with the sun shining through it.' She wanted to tell him to stop, but her mouth seemed to be glued shut. 'Perhaps it's the way your hair has been lightened that makes the difference.'

'Perhaps it is,' she said, making a supreme effort to move. 'Shall we—?'

But he hadn't finished. 'The dress was a good choice, too. Take off your coat—' She ignored him, instead buttoning it firmly over the cleavage that a few moments earlier she had been congratulating herself upon.

'Harriet suggested it,' she said, in an attempt to distract him. He was not distracted.

'Harriet was right. You have that luscious kind of figure that looks better when it is revealed rather than hidden beneath layers of clothing—'

'Max—' He was teasing her and she didn't want him to do that. She desperately didn't want him to. But the warning note in her voice went unheeded.

'And the shoes were a good choice.' He was looking at the embroidered toes peeping out from beneath the hem of her dress. Jilly began to relax. Shoes were safe enough. She could handle shoes. 'I did notice what pretty feet you have when you were trying them on. Pretty ankles too.' And then without warning he was looking directly into her eyes. 'But that's only to be expected when they are attached to the kind of legs that give men wet dreams...' Jilly's face flamed '...especially since you have this habit of opening your door wearing nothing but a T-shirt that barely covers—'

'Very funny, Max.'

'Funny?'

'You've had your little joke.' Jilly made a fairly mirthless attempt at a laugh. 'Now shall we go?'

'Who said I was joking?' For a moment Max remained perfectly still, looking at her in the kind of way that made her think, just for a moment, that he was going to kiss her, kiss her as if he really meant it and then rewrite any plans he had made for the evening. Her lips seemed to swell and burn with the thought and in that moment she knew exactly what had been happening to her. She didn't want to go anywhere tonight except to bed with Max Fleming, while all he was interested in was parcelling her up like a Christmas box for Richie Blake.

And as if to demonstrate just how stupid she was being, he turned away, picked up her evening bag and handed it to her.

'Thank you.' She flipped it open, ostensibly to check that she had everything she would need, but in reality to avoid meeting his eyes, to have something to do with her shaking fingers. Her shaking body would have to look after itself.

'Checking you haven't forgotten the contingency funds?' he enquired.

Jilly, determined to get a grip of herself, made herself look up at him. This was like that first morning when she had arrived in the office and, even without Amanda Garland's warning, she had known that the only way to handle Max Fleming was head on. So she raised her lashes and looked him full in the eyes. 'Why would I need them when I'm with you, Max?'

For once he seemed to have no answer and after a moment said, 'If you're ready, Jilly, shall we go?' His voice had lost its warmth, its unexpectedly teasing quality. Formality was back in place as he led the way down the steps into the courtyard and then offered her his arm. She would rather not have taken it. She wasn't quite sure why, but she just knew that even through the thickness of his coat and her own she would feel that heat.

She avoided it by stopping to look at a clump of snowdrops blooming beneath the bare branches of a shrub. He stopped, waited. 'I love snowdrops,' she said, feeling slightly silly.

He stared at them for a moment, then looked up. 'I hadn't noticed them. Charlotte... She must have planted them.' He took her arm. 'This way.' The silence lengthened as they walked around the house towards the front gate, broken only by the sound of his cane hitting the path with painful regularity.

'I see you're not taking any chances tonight,' Jilly said brightly, after a moment, trying to get back to where they had been a few minutes earlier. He glanced down at her. 'You've brought the magic wand.'

Max lifted the ebony cane, held it straight in front of him, regarding it thoughtfully as he opened the front gate for her. 'You never know when a little magic will come in handy.' With a bit of luck, he thought, it might even make Rich Blake disappear. 'After you, Miss Prescott.'

The driver was holding the car door open for them. 'This is so civilised,' Jilly said, once they were under way, and determined to divert the conversation to safer ground. 'No worries about parking, or drinking—'

'No worry that the leg might give way?' Max interjected smoothly.

'I didn't mean—' she began. Then, 'Is that why you don't drive?' Oh, heck. 'I'm sorry, I shouldn't—'

'It's just a gammy knee, Jilly. I could, I do drive an automatic when I'm in the country, but I don't see the point of keeping a car in London these days. There really is no need to be embarrassed about mentioning it.'

'My mother would have said I was being "personal".'

'Would she?' Max glanced at her, found it difficult not to smile. 'What's she like? Your mother?'

Jilly shrugged. 'She's just my mother. Middle-aged, overweight—'

'What does she think of Richie?'

'And over-protective,' she concluded meaningfully.

'Ah, well, all mothers are like that—even mine.' She glanced at him uncertainly. He must have seen her doubtful expression because he laughed. 'I do have a mother, Jilly. Would you like to meet her?' He didn't wait for her answer. 'I'll take you to lunch with her tomorrow, if you like.'

'You can't do that!' she exclaimed, horrified. 'What'll she think?'

Too much. 'That it's too long since I made the effort and she won't hesitate to say so.'

'About me. She'll have seen the paper too, won't she?'

'Unlikely, but I should think she's been getting phone calls all day from friends who have. So, it really would be a kindness to let her meet you.' Jilly looked doubtful. 'Don't worry. If she dislikes you she won't let it show.'

'So how will I know?'

'If she likes you she'll tell you that she warned me against marrying Charlotte.' He paused. 'Mothers are quite often right, you know—even the over-protective ones. But who ever listens to them?' And then he leaned forward, his hand on her shoulder. 'Look, there's Windsor Castle,' he said, while she was still struggling to think of some answer.

It was floodlit, its massive bulk seeming almost to float in the darkness. 'It's so big!' she exclaimed. 'I'd love to see inside now they've restored it. And the doll's house. My mother saw it once. All those tiny things, little books, wine bottles—'

'All filled with the real thing,' he assured her. 'You like miniature things? That settles it, then—tomorrow we'll have lunch with my mother and we'll walk around the castle in the afternoon.' Jilly still looked uncertain. 'Trust me, it'll be fine.'

The driver took a slip-road off the motorway and Jilly,

still unsure what to say, looked about her. 'Where are we going?'

'To a restaurant on the river near Maidenhead. Lovely food. You'll like it.'

'How do you know that Richie will be there?'

'Richie?' Max was beginning to wonder if she ever thought about anything else. 'He won't be.' At least he sincerely hoped not. He had the feeling that a little of Rich Blake would go a very long way. Then, seeing her confusion, 'Running into him two days in a row would be just a little obvious, don't you think? You wouldn't want him to think you were chasing him?'

'Oh, no. I'm sorry…'

Nowhere near as sorry as he was. 'For heaven's sake, do stop apologising, Jilly. I should have told you where we're going.' Irritability threatened to settle on his shoulders and they continued the journey in silence. What on earth was he doing? He stared out into the darkness as they sped through country lanes, but the darkness offered no answers.

Twenty minutes later they came to a halt outside an old inn beside the river. There were no photographers hanging about outside, but inside a restaurant that oozed with money Max was greeted with deference, and Jilly was aware of a definite rustle of interest as they made their way into a low, oak-beamed bar built centuries earlier and were shown to a table near the comforting warmth of a log fire. Heads turning. But, despite Max's promise that she would be making heads turn, she knew better than to take the credit.

What had it said in the newspaper that Harriet had shown her?

Max Fleming, who has been something of a recluse since the tragic death of his wife in a skiing accident, was last night seen on the town with Miss Jilly Prescott. One-time playboy, Max has been sorely missed at his old haunts and we hope the advent on the scene of the lovely Jilly means that we will be seeing more of him.

He had described himself as a man with more money than sense, and the newspaper confirmed his reputation as a playboy. Except that these days he worked, for no reward, with international agencies seeking solutions to Third World poverty. Whatever happened to his wife had clearly changed him deeply. So what was he doing here, with her?

She glanced at him as he asked the waiter to bring her an orange juice and a long gin and tonic for him.

'You did say you would be sticking to orange juice,' he reminded her, when she gave him what her mother would have described as an old-fashioned look. The drinks arrived along with vast menus. She did not take one. 'You'd better order dinner for me too, pet,' she advised him, her voice slipping easily into her regional dialect, 'since I'm only playing at being grown up to-night.'

Her flash of irritability reminded Max that beneath this elegant woman there was still a blunt northern lass and somewhere inside his head he smiled. 'It will be my pleasure. I hope you like French food.'

'I've no idea. Mayonnaise instead of salad cream is about as French as it gets where I come from.'

He didn't believe that for a moment. She was just cross with him for not treating her like the adult she was and he didn't blame her. She had paused now, but he sensed there was more so he waited. He was right.

'Perhaps you would like to educate me, Max?'

'Educate you?' He knew that something was on her mind, but she had nevertheless taken him by surprise. 'What about?'

'About French food, for a start. Then we can graduate to which knife and fork to use. You see, I've just worked out who you are, Max, or rather what you're playing at. Not the demon king. Not my fairy godfather. You're Professor Higgins and I'm your Eliza Doolittle.' And her heart was doing a fine job of breaking.

Max was shocked. She couldn't have been more wrong, but he doubted she would believe him if he told her so. 'That's an interesting theory, Jilly, but I have no desire to change the way you speak.' He loved that lilting accent, warm, full of character.

She was not convinced. 'You will. After all,' she pointed out, 'we've done the hair, the make-up, the clothes—'

'If this is about ordering your drink without consulting you, may I remind you that this morning you told me that you would be sticking to orange juice in future? I assumed you meant it. Was I wrong?'

'Orange juice was a generic term to cover any and all kinds of non-alcoholic drinks,' she said. 'Straight tonic, ginger ale, fizzy water.' She shrugged. 'Shall I go on?'

'I'd rather you didn't and I apologise for being particularly dense. What would you like to drink, Jilly?'

She picked up the orange juice and sipped it. Freshly squeezed. Delicious. 'This is fine.'

It was his turn to dispense the old-fashioned look. 'Good, because I would rather you kept a clear head this evening.' Her forehead creased in a puzzled frown. 'I don't want to be responsible for any regrets you might have later.'

'Regrets?'

'After Richie's seen you in that dress.'

'I thought we were avoiding Richie.'

'We can try. I can't guarantee it. London is a surprisingly small place.'

'I see.' Her expression hardly changed, yet as Jilly rose to her feet Max was in no doubt that she was seriously angry. 'Tell me, Max, are you suggesting that all it will take is one leer from Richie before I leap into bed with him?'

Jilly's lilting voice carried without effort and several people seated nearby half turned until, meeting Max's discouraging expression, they decided that they were not that interested after all.

'You're telling me that you haven't already?' Jilly might not have lowered her voice, but his was so low that it seemed to vibrate against her backbone.

She flushed, deep red. Then she leaned forward and for one heart-stopping moment he thought that she was going to return the orange juice after all, by the shortest route. But she replaced the glass on the table and picked up her bag. 'This,' she said, 'appears to be one of those contingencies you keep warning me about. I'll see you on Monday, Max. Nine o'clock. In the office. Don't be late.' Then she turned and, head high, swept out of the bar.

Jilly was shaking by the time she reached the ladies' cloakroom. She was miles from London and had no idea how to get back there short of calling a taxi. Somehow she didn't think Max's twenty-pound note would cover it and this wasn't the kind of place that would have a regular bus service passing the door.

She couldn't think what had come over her. Except that she didn't want Max thinking that she was easy, cheap, desperate to jump into bed with Richie like some groupie, just because he had made it, was a celebrity. She had never wanted to jump into bed with him at all, she realised, now she had been forced to confront the question. She didn't know what she *had* wanted. Just to be acknowledged, perhaps. For Richie to say…thank you. To treat her like the friend she had been to him.

There was only one man she wanted to share a bed with and… Oh, damn! She struggled with the catch on her bag, fumbled for a handkerchief, blotted away a stupid, ridiculous tear that was threatening to undo all that fancy make-up.

She needed to catch her breath, think, but, aware that several women had turned at her precipitate entrance, she turned quickly to a mirror and fiddled with her hair. Then she retouched her lipstick. Then she decided that there was no point in wasting any more time. She'd better get her coat. His coat. His dead wife's coat. The coat of the woman he should never have married, according to his mother. Who had been unhappy. Who had planted snowdrops. Why did that hurt so much?

She looked down at the dress she was wearing and vowed that it would go to the charity shop on Monday with the rest of the clothes she had borrowed. And the shoes. She looked down at her feet, the pretty embroidered shoes, the kind of shoes that she would never be able to afford to buy for herself, and she groaned.

CHAPTER NINE

Jilly stopped abruptly when she saw Max leaning against the wall, chatting to the cloakroom attendant. 'Ah, there you are, darling,' he said, his voice as smooth as heavy cream, one corner of his mouth lifted in a smile that looked like trouble. 'I thought you'd got lost. Our table is ready and the chef will commit murder if we allow his exquisite food to spoil.' And before she could tell him what he and the murderous chef could do with his table and his food, he had taken her arm and she was being propelled towards the dining room with a determination that left only the tips of her toes making contact with the ground.

Short of screaming 'Kidnap', 'Abduction' and making a scene of epic proportions, she had no choice but to go with him.

She might have been tempted, but somehow she knew that Max would handle a scene, no matter how epic, with consummate ease. So she forced herself to relax and the firm grip on her arm was immediately reduced to nothing more than a gentlemanly hand at her elbow.

They were bowed into the low-ceilinged dining room and shown to a table which overlooked the blackly gleaming river. A candle flickered, the light splintered by the crystal glasses, sparking off the heavy silverware. Max stood while the waiter held her chair, then, when she was safely seated, he took the chair opposite her. 'Now, darling,' he said, in the same smooth tones, 'would you like to tell me what the hell that was all about?'

Darling? She didn't much care for a term of endearment that was used as an insult, but perhaps she had deserved it. So what should she do? Apologise? Explain? How would he react if she told him that she no longer cared whether Richie took any notice of her, that only he mattered? No, she definitely would not be explaining…

'Tell me, Max, all that macho, assertive stuff…did it impress the ladies back in the days when you were a playboy?' She caught a fleeting look of surprise cross his features, then he threw back his head and laughed. Jilly hadn't known quite what sort of reaction she might provoke. Laughter was unexpected, but the sound was warm, special, and she found herself joining in. 'Well?'

'Jilly, behave yourself.'

'I don't want to behave myself.' Not one bit. 'You seem to think I'm incapable of it.' That stopped the laughter, she noticed. 'According to today's newspaper you were a playboy.' She regarded him over the candles and the flowers, his face all hard planes and dangerous shadows. 'You'll forgive me if I find that difficult to believe.'

'Yes, well, it was a while ago. Youthful excess.' So, it was true. And actually it wasn't that hard to believe, not when he smiled, really smiled as he was doing right now. 'And the answer to your question is yes.' For a moment she couldn't think what her question had been. She couldn't think at all. 'All that macho assertiveness impressed the hell out of the ladies.'

'Oh.' At least in the candlelight he couldn't see her blush. 'What happened?'

'You want a blow-by-blow description of every one of my youthful indiscretions?' he enquired.

'No.' At least, maybe she did. But not now. 'I mean why did you stop?'

'I did what all men eventually do. I stopped chasing a lot of women and concentrated on one…' Max nodded to a waiter hovering at a discreet distance and he poured the wine into two glasses. 'I do hope you are not going to object to my choice of wine. It's rather a favourite.'

She just stared at him, then the glass at her right hand. 'Why would I do that? After all, I won't be drinking it, will I?' She poured herself a glass of water from the jug on the table.

'Take no notice of me, Jilly. You have as much right to mess your life up as anyone else—in fact, since I'm doing my level best to help you, lecturing you on the subject is thoroughly stupid. Shall we eat, instead?' He moved to pick up a fork, but she reached out, covered his hand with hers.

'Max…'

Max held his breath, scarcely caring what she was about to say, only feeling the cool touch of her fingers against his, only intent upon keeping in check the bewildering urge driving him to turn his hand, seize hers and hold on to it, never let it go.

'I haven't said thank you.'

He wasn't sure what he had been hoping for, but it wasn't her thanks. 'Don't be too quick to thank me, I'm doing you no favours.' And he glanced pointedly at her hand. She withdrew it quickly, self-consciously, and Max had to struggle not to reach out and take it back, tell her that she was making the biggest mistake of her life.

He resisted. He had married Charlotte against the advice of his family, his friends. Unwanted advice was just a waste of breath. But maybe Jilly was right, maybe lunch with his mother was not such a good idea. Maybe none of this was. Maybe he should end it all as quickly as possible. 'Excuse me, Jilly.' He extracted a pen from his pocket and a slender notebook and swiftly wrote a note, folded it. A glance brought a waiter. 'Will you give this to my driver, please?' The man departed, and when Max finally picked up his fork he was pleased to note that his hand wasn't shaking noticeably. It was just about the only part of him that wasn't.

'Now this, Jilly,' he said, in the earnest lecturing tone of a teacher, 'is a mosaic of pheasant, rabbit and *foie gras* with pickled *girolles*—'

Jilly, who had been regarding the beautifully prepared and presented food that had been set before her with an intensity that had more to do with avoiding looking at Max than hunger, finally looked up. 'Is that right? Well, isn't education a wonderful thing?' She flicked out her napkin and laid it upon her lap. 'Now, you see, *I'd* have said it was posh pâté with some funny looking mushrooms on the side.'

'And you'd be right.' He caught her eye and grinned. For a moment a smile wavered uncertainly about her lips, then won. The internal shaking intensified but he raised his glass to her. '*Pax?*' he offered.

'French, Latin…you playboys really know how to show a girl a good time.'

'As I said, I'm out of practice, Jilly, but I'll do my best.'

Out of practice, her left foot. Flirtation came to him as naturally as breathing. 'In that case…' and she picked up her glass of water and touched it against his… '*Pax* it is.'

'Tell me about your home, Jilly. Your family. You have an over-protective mother...' He left it for her to continue.

'My mother works for the library service. She drives a van load of books around to the old folks, making sure they get their Catherine Cookson and Dick Francis.'

'Brothers? Sisters?'

'I've two younger brothers. Michael is seventeen and determined to make a million developing computer software by the time he's twenty. George is more interested in playing football.'

'And he wants to play for Newcastle, of course.'

'Who else? I could have bought him the new club strip with the money I spent on shoes and a lipstick today.'

'And your father? Like Rich Blake's father, I think you said, not a candidate for father of the year.'

'No, he was never that.' The first course had been cleared away and Jilly was spinning the stem of her glass between her fingers, watching the light from the candle glow through the water. 'My mother left him when George was a baby.'

'Another woman?'

She shook her head, still staring at the glass. Then she gave a little shiver. 'He used to hit her. The last time was because George was crying and Mum couldn't get him to stop.' She flinched even as she told him. 'I took George and Michael and hid with them in a cupboard. He was too drunk to work out where we were.' She swallowed. 'Mum wouldn't tell him.'

He saw her remembering, hearing what had happened, and he reached out, grasped her wrist. 'You don't have to go on.'

But she did. 'Next day Mum packed what she could

and she took us to a refuge. Eventually the magistrate made a court order excluding my father from the house and we went home. He'd smashed everything. Every cup, every glass, every plate. And he'd taken an axe to the furniture. But he never came back.' Then, 'I've never told anyone else that.' She looked up. 'Not even Richie.'

He was shaken. Fit to kill. He wanted to take her and hold her and promise that nothing would ever hurt her again. Instead he said, 'It's hardly surprising that your mother is protective. You're lucky that she was strong enough to get out.'

'Strong?' Jilly had never thought of her mother as strong. She'd taken the beatings for years, they had all taken the beatings; it had only been fear that he would kill George that had finally driven her from the house.

'It's hard to leave with no money, nowhere to go. A lot of women find it impossible,' Max said gently. 'Never get out.'

'Yes,' she said, astonished that he had been able to see what she never had. 'I suppose I am lucky.'

More food arrived. 'Roast sea bass,' Max said matter-of-factly. 'I hope you like fish; I should have asked. I'm not having a very good night.'

'I don't believe I gave you a chance, Max. I'm sorry. I know you were only trying to protect me but it really isn't necessary. I've known Richie for a very long time, I know all his faults—'

'Not all of them, or you wouldn't have allowed him to smother you in psychedelic goo for the amusement of fifteen million viewers the other night.' She didn't answer. 'You don't seriously expect me to believe that you came all the way from Newcastle just to hold hands with him, do you, Jilly? I saw you after that television show, remember?'

For a moment she tried to stare him down, then her gaze dropped to the roast sea bass and, without another word, she picked up her fork.

Max watched her for a moment as she concentrated one hundred per cent on her food. It had been his intention to string this performance out over a week or so, to drive Blake crazy, but if she was in love with the man then he had no right to be playing games.

'How is that?' he asked.

'Delicious.' Then, politely, 'Thank you.'

Oh, God. How on earth had he got himself into something like this? She was so vulnerable that he wanted to wrap her in cotton wool and take her home, hold her and keep her safe for ever. Instead he said, 'Eat it all up and I'll let you choose your own pudding.'

It was after ten-thirty when they returned to the car. 'Did you find him?' Max asked the driver as Jilly climbed in.

'He arrived at the Rivi Club with a party of friends about five minutes ago. I've booked a table.'

'Well, Jilly, you'll be dancing the night away with a vengeance tonight.'

'What about your knee?'

He gave her one of those old-fashioned looks.

'You did say that I wasn't to be embarrassed about mentioning it.'

'Maybe I did, but please don't make it your first concern. I'll be fine. And if I'm not, well, you seem to have an instant cure.' Her forehead creased in a frown. 'Magic lips, Jilly. Kissing it better really works.'

It was the first time either of them had referred to that kiss and for a moment neither of them moved, then Jilly swallowed hard and said, 'Any time. Just say the word.'

*   *   *

The Rivi Club was jumping by the time they arrived and they had to squeeze through the tightly packed tables to reach the one set aside for Max. It occurred to Jilly that Max Fleming must have been one heck of a playboy if all it had taken was a telephone call from his chauffeur to get a table exactly where he wanted it on a Saturday night.

Max, tall, darkly good-looking, attracted the first attention from the table next to them. Petra recognised him from the previous night and immediately pointed him out to Richie, and then they both looked at her. Then Richie stood up. 'Jilly?' he said, crossing over to her.

'Hi, Richie,' she said.

'What have you done to your hair? I wouldn't have recognised you.' She'd forgotten how different she looked. Richie didn't wait for an answer. 'Hello, Max. Why don't you come and join us?'

Jilly didn't want to do any such thing, in fact she thought Max had planned to keep him at a distance, but instead he shrugged. 'Why not?' he said. And then she saw why. A girl with a slashed-to-the-waist dress was giving him a look that would have fried an egg; perhaps that was why Jilly accepted Richie's invitation to dance with an eagerness she was far from feeling. Max, his eyes fastened to a dress that revealed more than it concealed, didn't seem to notice.

'God, Jilly, you look great,' Richie said. A week ago those words would have sent her into the stratosphere, now she didn't care. She looked around him. Petra was watching them through narrowed eyes and Jilly had a sudden insight into how she was feeling, felt a pang of sympathy.

'Richie, are you and Petra…' Her mother would have said 'courting', a deliciously old-fashioned expression that would cover every possible combination of relation-ship, but Richie picked up on her meaning and grinned.

'Yeah, we've been living together for six months. She's a great girl.'

Jilly waited for some feeling of hurt. None came. 'You mean she does everything I used to and you get the sex, too?'

He seemed slightly startled by her directness. 'Well, it never was like that for us, was it? We're friends.'

'Yes, Richie. We're friends. Although if you ever pull a stunt like that goo trick on me again I'll tell the whole world about the time you locked yourself in the lavatory and cried.'

'You wouldn't!'

'Don't count on it.'

For a moment he stared at her and then burst out laughing. 'God, Jilly, I've missed you,' he said, and hugged her.

Max hadn't taken his eyes off them and as Rich Blake wrapped his arms about Jilly, pulled her close and hugged her, he knew he couldn't stay for another mo-ment and watch the man reclaim her. He took his pen from his jacket pocket and wrote a brief note on a paper napkin. 'Petra.' She turned and it occurred to him that she looked as miserable as he felt. 'Would you give Jilly this for me?'

'You're leaving?'

'My knee is playing up,' he said. 'I don't want to spoil her evening and I know Richie will see her safely home.'

'Max, darling, will you see *me* home? I'm not in the least bit bothered about the safe bit…' The girl with her cleavage spilling out all over the table was looking at him with the kind of eyes that might once have offered some temptation.

Instead he turned to where Jilly was dancing, for a moment watched the way her body gyrated to the music, her arms held high as she swayed and turned and laughed at something Richie said to her.

Then he turned back to the girl beside him. 'Of course…' He tried to recall her name, but not very hard, he wasn't that interested. She couldn't quite believe it when he saw her to her door and left her there, politely refusing her offer of a nightcap.

Jilly was still laughing as she returned to their table and flopped into her chair, shaking her head as someone filled a champagne glass and offered it to her. Then Petra passed her a napkin. 'Max left you this,' she said.

'Max? Why? Where's he gone?'

'He said something about his knee playing up.' But Jilly had already opened the folded napkin. He'd written, 'Good luck. Max.' She turned it over as if she might have missed something. 'He took Lisa home,' Petra added, with just a hint of spite. 'Perhaps she offered to massage it for him. Or something.'

'Lisa?' Jilly glanced around. 'Who's Lisa?' It was then she realised exactly who Lisa was. Exactly what Max had meant. Not just good luck, but goodbye. Forget Windsor. Forget lunch with his mother. He had seen her dancing with Richie and, job done, it hadn't taken him long to find someone else to distract him. Someone else to be photographed with for the morning paper. It might have been a while since he had been a regular playboy, but perhaps it was like riding a bicycle, something you never quite lost the knack of. For a moment Jilly stared unseeing at the glass in front of her and then she picked it up and drained it.

* * *

Richie insisted on seeing Jilly to her door. It was well after two in the morning and on the outside she was a giggling mess who couldn't quite handle the door key, but inside everything was very still and cold because no matter how much champagne she had drunk the coldness and the emptiness hadn't gone away.

'You're going to have a devil of a head in the morning, Jilly. Are you sure you'll be all right?' Richie pushed the key into the lock and helped her inside. 'I don't like to leave you on your own.'

'I'll be fine. Really.'

'Sit there. Let me make you some coffee.'

'There's no need. You can't leave Petra in the car.'

'She'll understand.' And he insisted she sat down while he made her a mug of black coffee, topping it up with cold water so that she could drink it quickly.

Across the courtyard Max was standing in the shadows behind one of the tall upper-storey windows. He'd heard the car arrive, watched Richie, arm about Jilly, walk her up the stone steps to the flat over the garage. He'd seen the door shut firmly behind them and the light go on. And then he'd drawn the curtain and shut out the view.

Despite shaky hands that rattled the mug against her teeth, Jilly could see that the only way to get rid of Richie was to do what he wanted and she drank the coffee as quickly as she could. There was so much of it. 'There,' she said at last, handing him the mug so that he could see for himself. 'All gone. Now it's your turn to go.'

He still wasn't convinced. 'Are you sure you're going to be all right? I could go and knock up Max—'

'No!' She stood up quickly. He might not be there;

she'd really rather not know. 'Please go, Richie. I'll be fine. Really.'

Richie scribbled a number on the cover of a magazine in front her. 'This is my home number—phone me in the morning.' She nodded, wished she hadn't and put her hand quickly to her forehead. 'Promise.'

'I promise. I'll phone. Just go. And be quiet or you'll wake the housekeeper.' She practically pushed him out of the door, then stood watching him make his way across the yard. He disappeared after a moment but she didn't immediately close the door. Instead she stood for a while staring across at the silent house. Even so late there was usually a light from the study window, a glow from the fire, where a sleepless Max would be working, but tonight everything was in darkness.

Very quietly she closed the door, peeled off the beautiful gown, removed her make-up, discarded everything that had made her feel so special tonight. She knew now that it was Max who had made her feel special. Only Max.

She should have told him. She shouldn't have let him go on thinking that she cared for Richie in that way. She'd pretended just to be near him and now he and his bad knee were with Lisa, and Lisa was kissing him better. All over, she shouldn't wonder.

She pulled on her sleep T-shirt and fell into bed. Her head was too fuddled to think about it right now, but in the morning she would sort it all out. Tomorrow was another day. Today was another day.

Jilly woke to the quiet of Sunday. Or as quiet as it ever got in London. There was a dull throbbing behind her eyes and her mouth felt like the back end of a sand dune, but apart from that everything seemed to be fine. And then she remembered and she wished she were still fast asleep.

But she wasn't, so she threw back the bedclothes, put on the kettle, took a couple of painkillers and consoled herself with the thought that she wasn't cut out for the fast lane. Except, of course, if she had stayed with Max last night she wouldn't have a headache, he'd have made certain of that.

That was when she noticed a square white envelope had been pushed under the door. She knew who it was from before she saw the writing. This was Max's personal stationery, the kind he used for handwritten notes. It simply said 'Jilly' on the envelope. She tugged at the flap, then read:

Dear Jilly,

I'm glad everything has worked out as you wanted. I'm sorry not to speak to you myself, but I've been called away so there is no need to feel bound by your promise to work until Laura returns. However, the flat is yours until the end of the month, should you need it. Please accept my warmest wishes for the future.

Max.

Warmest wishes? What about that kiss? That hadn't been warm, that had been hot. And the way he had danced with her? Held her?

She stared at the note she was holding. Polite, formal and unmistakably goodbye. She couldn't believe it. She wouldn't believe it. Lisa couldn't have been that great. Could she?

She flung on her jogging pants and sweatshirt, pushed

her feet into her trainers and ran across the courtyard to the kitchen. Harriet looked up from preparing vegetables for lunch. 'Where is he?'

'Max?' Harriet looked uncomfortable. 'I thought he left you a note explaining that he's been called away.'

'Where to? I want to speak to him.'

'He's gone to Strasbourg, there's some EC committee meeting first thing tomorrow. He spoke to Ms Garland before he left. If you call in at her office tomorrow she'll pay you and sort you out another job if you need it.'

Jilly suddenly felt very foolish. What on earth was she doing demanding to speak to Max as if she were anything more than a temporary secretary?

'Can I make you some lunch, Jilly?'

'What?' She stared at the bowl of carrots and potatoes waiting to be cooked. 'You've done a lot for one.'

'For one?' Harriet, too, stared at the vegetables. 'I suppose I have. Will you stay?'

'Oh, no. Thank you, Harriet. I'll be leaving today. Moving out. I'll leave everything tidy.' She paused. 'Thank you for everything you've done for me. I've really enjoyed working here.' Then, 'I'm sorry to have missed Max.'

'One of those emergencies…you know.'

'Yes, I know. I'll leave Mrs Fleming's clothes in the flat, Harriet. If you could see that they are passed on to the charity shop.'

'Of course.'

'I'll drop the keys in later.'

'Just push them through the letterbox if you're in a hurry.'

Jilly nodded and left the kitchen. For a moment Harriet watched her, then turned as Max rejoined her in the kitchen.

'What would you have done if she'd accepted your invitation to lunch, Harriet?'

'More to the point, what would you have done?' She turned and looked at him. 'You're a fool to let her go, Max.'

He shook his head. 'Fools are men who don't learn from their mistakes. Charlotte might not have been any happier if I hadn't married her, but she would almost certainly be alive.'

Jilly looked around her. She'd stripped the bed, cleaned the little flat until it shone and packed all her belongings in her shabby old suitcase. Charlotte Fleming's lovely clothes were neatly folded and awaiting Harriet's attention. There was nothing left to do except go home. She picked up her suitcase and walked out onto the steps, turning to lock the door behind her. The telephone began to ring.

For a moment she was absolutely still, riveted to the spot. Then she pushed the key back into the lock, her hand shaking as she tried to turn it, terrified that the ringing would stop before she could reach the telephone. It was Richie.

'You promised you'd ring, Jilly, are you all right?'

There was a moment when she struggled hard to breathe, to contain the bitter disappointment, fight back the tears. 'Yes, Richie.'

'You're sure, bonny lass? You don't sound too good.'

'Nothing that a couple of aspirin won't fix,' she said. 'I guess I'm not built for all this fast living.'

'You won't be up to a party tonight, then?'

'Another one?'

'It's a bit special. Petra and I have decided to get married.'

'That's wonderful news, Richie.'

'Will you come, then? Petra asked me to ring you. She'd like to say sorry for not being kinder. She was jealous...'

'I understand, Richie. Tell her that from me. But I'm going home. You just caught me—I'm on my way to the station, right now. I don't think I'm cut out for London.'

'Really? I thought you and Max—' He stopped. 'Well, you always did know your own mind, pet. Give my best to your mother.'

Oh, sure, her mother would love that. 'Richie... Take care of Petra. You need someone like her, you know.'

He chuckled. 'Everything you did and the sex too. I know.'

'Don't hurt her, Richie. You need to have your feet on the ground in your business.'

'Still dishing out the good advice wholesale, are you? Look, pet, don't catch the train. Let me organise a car to take you home in style. It's the least I can do after what happened on Friday night.'

About to refuse, Jilly paused. It was Sunday, a bad day to travel with long delays for maintenance work on the track, long hours in a noisy train. And he was right. It was the least he could do. 'Thanks, Richie.'

Harriet answered the gate bell fifteen minutes later and a disembodied voice said, 'Mr Blake's car for Miss Prescott.'

'You'll find her in the flat over the garage,' Harriet said, and released the lock. Then she turned and saw Max standing in the study doorway.

'Will she be bringing the keys over?' he said.

'She brought them ten minutes ago. She didn't come in, just pushed them through the door. There's still time to catch her—' But he had already closed the study door.

CHAPTER TEN

AMANDA GARLAND sifted through the papers on her desk. 'Beth, have we had a time sheet from Jilly Prescott for last week?'

'Not yet. Between the working hours your brother keeps and the nightclubbing I don't suppose she's had time.'

'I don't care how busy she is, it's Friday and it should have been in days ago. Call her, will you? No, wait. I'll do it.' She lifted the receiver and dialled her brother's office.

'Max Fleming's office, Laura Graham speaking.'

'Laura? What on earth are you doing there?' The words were shocked out of her. 'How's your mother?' she added quickly.

'About the same, but Max couldn't cope without me any longer so he hired a nurse to look after her just to have me in a few hours a day. You know how he is with temps—'

Amanda raised her eyes briefly to the ceiling. Laura Graham might be indispensable, but did she have to constantly remind everyone of the fact? 'I don't understand, Laura. Where's Jilly?'

'Jilly? Jilly Prescott? She left last Sunday, didn't you know?' The woman was so damned *smug*! 'She moved in with her boyfriend, apparently. Some television person. I assumed she'd been in touch about getting paid. Max told her to. Maybe she doesn't need the money...'

'Let me speak to Max.'

'He's on the other line. To be honest, Amanda, both Harriet and I are extremely worried about him.' As if *she* didn't worry about him? 'He's not eating properly—in fact he's scarcely eating at all, but then I suppose you know that—'

'No, of course I didn't know. I thought… I hoped… Oh, damn the girl.' Then, 'Oh, no. That's not fair, it's not her fault, it isn't anybody's fault. I knew it would all end in tears.' She sighed. 'Have you got a forwarding address for her, Laura?'

'She left nothing, except some shoes. Harriet wanted to send them on, but Max said he didn't have her address.'

'Well, send them over to me. I have her address on file somewhere. I'll speak to you again soon, Laura.' She replaced the receiver, looked at Beth. 'You'd better ring Rich Blake's office and find out where Jilly Prescott wants me to send her cheque.'

'Rich Blake? Why on earth would he know?'

'Just do it, Beth. Now,' she added when Beth hesitated.

'I'd better leave it until Monday.' Amanda stared at her. 'There won't be anyone there today. At least, not anyone sober enough to answer a question sensibly.'

'And why not?'

'Haven't you seen the paper?' Amanda Garland looked up as her secretary offered her the early edition of the evening paper. 'Rich Blake got married this morning.'

'What?'

'"Secret Wedding of TV Star. Rich Blake marries in the most secret wedding of the year." Don't they write a load of tosh? I don't know what was so secret about it. There were obviously dozens of people there, including the photographer from this newspaper.'

Amanda snatched the paper from her secretary, scanned the picture. 'I don't understand. This isn't Jilly.'

'Jilly? Jilly Prescott? Why would he marry her when he's been living with Petra James for months?'

'But Max thought that Rich Blake and Jilly...' She stopped. 'So where is Jilly?' She didn't wait for an answer; she knew. 'What a prize pair of idiots. Get me Jilly's file. No, I'll get it myself.' She snatched the file from the cabinet and headed for the door. Then she scooted back to pick up the newspaper.

'Where are you going? What about your three o'clock appointment?' Beth shouted after her.

'You deal with it.' The traffic was backed up for miles and in a fit of impatience Amanda paid off her taxi and ran the rest of the way, leaning breathlessly on the bell when she reached her brother's gate. Harriet let her in but she didn't stop to say hello. 'Max! Where are you?'

Max turned as Amanda appeared in the doorway of Laura's office. 'Mandy?' His sister, that temple to grooming and poise, was breathless and dishevelled. 'What on earth is the matter with you?'

'With me?' She stared at him. His skin was grey and pallid and he looked thinner than ever. 'There's nothing whatever the matter with me.' She thrust the newspaper into his hand. 'Look at that.' She saw him take in the headline, physically flinch. It was all she needed. 'It isn't Jilly, Max. Don't you understand? It's not Jilly.' Then, 'Max? Where are you going?'

'Where do you think?' he said as he headed for the front door. 'I'm going to find her, find out what the hell is going on—'

'Don't you want her address?' She opened the file she

was clutching and held out the letter that Jilly had written when she had sent her CV. He took it in hands that were visibly shaking. Held it. Amanda grinned, gave him a push. 'What are you waiting for, big brother?'

'Just for this.' And he gave her a bone-crushing hug before turning and heading for the door.

Laura appeared in the doorway. 'Where's Max gone?'

'To find Jilly.' Harriet, who hadn't moved from the doorway since Amanda burst in, was grinning broadly.

Amanda beamed too. 'Isn't it romantic?'

Laura simply raised a pair of disapproving eyebrows. 'Madness, more like. He hasn't taken his cane. Or his coat. He's bound to catch his death of cold.'

Jilly hesitated before pushing open the door of the Garland Agency. She desperately needed the money she had earned working for Max, but to see his sister, be so close, was almost unbearable. But she had quickly learned that it was unbearable wherever she was; at least here in London she was in the same city as him. And Amanda had said she could find her work any time. Maybe if she stayed she might even see him…

Beth turned as she walked into the office, stared at her blankly. 'Jilly.'

'I was in London today,' she said awkwardly, placing her time sheet on the desk. 'At a wedding. Max said if I dropped by you'd organise a cheque for me. I'm sorry I didn't send my time sheet—'

'Have you seen Max?' Beth asked.

'Not since last Saturday.' She turned as Amanda followed her into the office.

'Jilly.' Amanda said her name in that same flat, unbelieving voice that Beth had used.

She glanced from one to the other. 'Is something wrong? What is it?'

'It's Max…'

Max? 'What about Max?' Anxiety sent adrenalin racing to every part of her, demanding that she run in five different directions at once, but she couldn't move a muscle, was frozen to the spot with dread. 'What's the matter with him? Is he ill? Hurt?'

'He's gone to Newcastle…'

Jilly's brow furrowed in a frown. Why on earth would Max have gone to Newcastle?

'He's gone to find *you*,' Amanda shouted. 'I thought— We both thought… Oh, Jilly, what on earth are you doing *here*?'

Jilly hadn't wanted to come to London for Richie's wedding, but he had begged her to, had even sent a car for her. It was as if he had needed her approval for this one last time. She had been planning to stay overnight with Gemma, now back from her Florida idyll and desperate to flaunt her tan…

And Max had chosen this moment to go to Newcastle to find her. To find *her*! For a moment she didn't know whether to laugh or cry. Then she knew exactly what to do and without another word she turned and headed for the door. 'What about your cheque?' Beth called after her.

'I can't wait. Send it on.'

'Where to?'

'Newcastle. Where else?'

Beth turned to Amanda. 'This Newcastle must be some place,' she said. 'Maybe you should open an office there.'

Max fumed through the traffic hold-up as the rush hour gathered pace, glancing at his watch every ten seconds as if that helped; he didn't even know what time the trains ran from King's Cross, or how often. He hadn't even stopped to pick up a mobile phone so that he could call and ask. He hadn't stopped for anything. Not even to think.

But perhaps he'd been doing too much thinking lately. Action suited him better and he drummed his fingers irritably as he stared out of the window at the stalled traffic, almost exploding with impatience at the delay, desperate to see Jilly, tell her all the things he should have told her, ask her to come back. Ask her...

Realising that he was staring at the entrance to the underground, he paid off the cabby and headed for the trains.

Jilly didn't have enough money for a cab—besides, looking at the gridlocked traffic it was obvious that the underground would be a better bet. She glanced at her watch. She was going to miss the four o'clock train but with luck and a good connection she might just make the four-thirty. She glanced at her watch again and the minutes seemed to have flown by so that she wished she had wings, could fly...

Why was Max going to Newcastle?

Amanda had said he was looking for *her*. But *why*?

There was a rush of air and the train rattled into the station. She leapt on, hanging onto a strap, too impatient to sit. She changed at Green Park, just missing a connection while she studied the map, tried to figure out whether she was heading north or south.

It was four twenty-five as she raced up the steps to the main station, staring at the departures board to find the platform, stumbling over piles of baggage, snagging her tights, cursing the high-heeled shoes and long straight skirt she'd worn for the wedding.

She reached the barrier just as it came down. She tried to duck around it, but the woman inspector stopped her. 'Too late, miss. There'll be another one in half an hour.'

'Please, can't you let me through?'

'Matter of life and death, is it?' she asked cynically.

'No,' Jilly said breathlessly. 'Love.'

Max settled himself in the window seat of the first class compartment with his newspaper. He'd made it with time to spare and now had three long hours in which to ponder the future. He had set off without thinking…only feeling. But then he'd been doing too much thinking during the last week, trying to do what Jilly wanted, what he'd thought she wanted.

Had she fled back home nursing a broken heart because Blake had chosen to marry someone else? Yet they had hugged like the best of friends and Blake had brought her home. He had been so certain… But surely Rich Blake couldn't be that much of a heel? No one could know Jilly and do that to her.

There was only one way to find out. And he had to find out.

Three hours. It stretched in front of him like three years. How on earth was he going to endure the wait?

'There's always one, isn't there?'

Max glanced at the man who had taken the seat opposite him. 'I beg your pardon?'

'Always one poor soul who just misses the train.' He nodded towards the barrier.

Max, to be polite, turned, saw an elegantly dressed young woman pleading with the guard to let her through. She was wearing a long dark overcoat, but it was the soft sweater spilling over the collar that caught his attention. It was peach. Like the one Jilly had bought. He continued to stare. 'Oh, my God. Jilly!'

'Love?' The woman's face split in a broad smile. 'Well, why didn't you say so?' She turned to the guard who was checking along the train to make certain all the doors were closed, and shouted out, 'Hold on, George. One more passenger here for the love train.' She lifted the barrier and let Jilly through. 'Go on, then. And give him a kiss from me.'

'No, they've taken pity on her. Who wouldn't with a smile like that?' The man turned back to Max. 'Sorry? Did you say something?'

Max couldn't believe it. Jilly was in Newcastle. Amanda had said so. How could she be here, on this train? He dropped his newspaper, struggled awkwardly to his feet and began walking towards the rear of the train.

'It doesn't hurt to be civil, you know,' the man called after Max. He didn't hear.

It had to be a mistake. It couldn't be her. It was just the colour that had caught his eye, the way her hair curled about her cheeks. He'd been the length of the train away, it was impossible to be sure. And yet he knew it was her. Somehow, incredibly, she was here...

It was Friday and the first carriage was full of students going home for the weekend and weekday exiles returning to the bosom of their families. Jilly began to make her way along the central aisle, hoping to find a seat further along the train.

It was slow going, the aisles were cluttered with people still settling in, taking off their coats, finding places for bulky rucksacks, glossy carriers full of shopping.

Max made his way slowly back through the train, checking every seat, looking for the special colour that had made her skin glow. He reached the buffet car and for a moment thought he had found her. But the girl in the queue waiting for the buffet to open turned as he approached and his heart, which for one giddy moment had soared, plummeted painfully as he realised his mistake. The girl was nothing like Jilly. Of course she wasn't. It was just that his mind had been focussed on her to the exclusion of everything else.

He turned back. Three hours.

'Tickets, please.'

'Oh, heavens, I haven't got one. I only just made the train by the skin of my teeth.' The voice, the lilting, honeyed accent, was unmistakable. Yet there must be dozens of girls on this train heading for home who spoke just like Jilly. He wouldn't allow himself to be fooled by wanting again. 'Am I in trouble?' Her voice was full of laughter. 'I couldn't wait, you see…'

Max turned, he couldn't help himself, and there she was standing in the entrance to the buffet, bending over her bag as she searched for her purse. 'Will you take a credit card?'

'Yes, miss. Where to?'

'Newcastle.'

'Single or return?'

She hesitated. 'I'm not sure…'

Max leaned over her shoulder, handed his own card to the conductor. 'Make that two first class tickets.'

Jilly spun round. 'Max!' It was there in her eyes. All the warmth, all the love. How had he ever missed it?

And suddenly there was no need to search for the right words, there was only the truth. 'I thought—'

'I was coming to find you, Jilly.'

'Amanda told me. I came down for Richie's wedding and I called in at the office and she told me...'

She *knew* about that and she didn't care?

'I thought you were hours ahead of me.'

And she'd come after him. The knowledge gave him courage, hope, belief...

'I need you, Jilly.'

'Need me?' Her eyes searched his. 'As your secretary?'

There was an expectant hush from the buffet car queue, the conductor.

'Laura's my secretary. I need you...' The words had come from deep within him, a deep, secret place where he had buried them in that moment when she had flung her arms about Rich Blake and hugged him. The kind of hug you'd give a friend? Unlike the kiss they had exchanged on the stairs at Spangles... 'I need you as my wife.'

Jilly thought perhaps she was dreaming. Just to love him, have him love her was enough. She knew how much such a commitment meant to him. 'Max...' Her voice could scarcely make it through a throat tight with the sudden need to weep. 'Oh, Max, are you sure?'

'Of course he's sure, pet,' someone said encouragingly. 'Can't you see that the man's in love?'

Max had meant to woo her slowly, take his time, show her how much he cared. He had learned enough to let her go when he'd thought that was what she wanted, now he had to learn to commute his longing for her, hold back, live with it patiently until she was ready to make a total commitment. Nothing less would do. 'I'm sure,' he said. 'But I'll wait until you are. No matter how long it takes.'

'Good grief, lass, put the man out of his misery, for pity's sake.'

Jilly's lips parted on an uncertain smile. 'I'm sure if you're sure.'

'Well, there you are, then. What are the pair of you waiting for? Give the girl a kiss, man.'

Max touched his hand to her cheek, but before he could gratefully accept this stranger's urging to do what he most longed to he was interrupted by a careful throat-clearing from the conductor.

'Excuse me, sir, but can you put this touching moment on hold while we decide exactly where you're going?'

Max didn't take his eyes off Jilly. 'Make that two tickets to paradise.'

'Paradise?' The conductor shook his head, but he was grinning. 'Right, sir.' He knew when to give in gracefully. 'And would that be single or return?'

'Single,' Max said without hesitation. 'We're never coming back.'

EPILOGUE

PARADISE. The small stone church bathed in sunlight and the beautiful Northumbrian countryside that stretched into the distance came close, Jilly decided, as her young brother took her hand and helped her from the wedding car.

Paradise. Max hadn't seen Jilly for three days. It had felt more like three years. The last three minutes had seemed like three years. Then there was a rustle of excitement from the church doorway, the vicar took his place and the organist struck up the wedding march, and he was on his feet while the congregation were still thinking about it.

She was framed for a moment in the doorway, a vision in white silk, his mother's diamonds holding the antique veil in place. And his heart seemed squeezed beneath his ribs as if there weren't quite enough room for it any more. There was the momentary distraction of a flutter of lace as his sister wiped a tear from her eye, a quick reassuring smile from his mother before she turned to watch Jilly's slow procession towards him. Then he stepped forward, took her hand.

'Marrying the boss is such a cliché, don't you think?'

Sarah Prescott, watching her daughter take her place beside Max at the altar, smiled at her sister. 'Is it?'

'He's older than she is, too.'

'Well, Jilly always was mature for her age.'

'And wasn't it all a bit of a rush? They've only known one another a few months.'

'Why would they wait? They're in love and, unlike most people, they don't have to save up for a deposit on a house.' Her smile deepened. She'd listened for years to her sister's tales of exotic foreign holidays, her husband's cars, Gemma's latest boyfriend. 'Did I tell you that Max has three?'

'Three?'

'Houses. Well, four if you count the villa in Tuscany.' Then, 'Your Gemma is such a pretty girl. I always thought she would be the first of them to get married. Still, she makes a lovely bridesmaid…'

'Dearly beloved, we are gathered together…'

Paradise. Vows made, rings exchanged, register signed and witnessed. As she emerged from the vestry on the arm of the man she loved, Jilly saw the massed flowers, friends and family packed in to wish them both well, all those things she had missed on that slow walk up the aisle when she had had eyes for no one but Max. She was so utterly happy and yet, for just a moment, she was assailed by panic. Life wasn't like this. It was too perfect. She was *too* happy…

Somehow they arrived at the doorway of the church, emerged blinking into the late spring sunshine. 'Jilly?' She looked up at the man beside her. 'Darling, what is it?' He placed a hand on the arm resting on his, his voice all concern. 'What's the matter?'

'Nothing.'

'Tell me.'

'I'm just being silly.' Except… 'How will we ever stay this happy, Max?'

He saw the flicker of doubt darken her eyes. Knew

that she was thinking that he must have been happy like this once before and that it had all gone tragically wrong.

'We won't.' *Won't?* Jilly had wanted reassurance… 'This is just the beginning. We've a lifetime of loving, of children, of memories to pile onto the way we feel now. The only limit to our happiness is our ability to imagine the possibilities.' He lifted her hand, kissed it. 'I want you to know that nothing I have ever done has been more right, more perfect.' He looked up, saw the photographer waiting, their families and friends eager to congratulate them. 'Come on, Mrs Fleming, it's time to get this marriage on the road before our guests expire for want of champagne and I expire for want of you. I've got two singles to paradise burning a hole in my pocket.'

'Newcastle? Again?'

'I had a good time in Newcastle.'

Jilly giggled. 'So did I, but I was hoping for somewhere just a bit more romantic for my honeymoon.'

'Then you won't be disappointed. Paradise is a moveable destination, as you're about to discover, Mrs Fleming. It's not where you are. It's who you're with.' And as he bent to kiss her the photographer took it as his cue to begin.

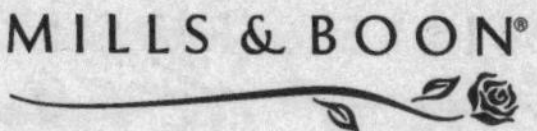

Next Month's Romance Titles

Each month you can choose from a wide variety of romance novels from Mills & Boon®. Below are the new titles to look out for next month from the Presents...™ and Enchanted™ series.

Presents...™

THE MISTRESS BRIDE	Michelle Reid
THE BLACKMAILED BRIDEGROOM	Miranda Lee
A HUSBAND OF CONVENIENCE	Jacqueline Baird
THE BABY CLAIM	Catherine George
THE MOTHER OF HIS CHILD	Sandra Field
A MARRIAGE ON PAPER	Kathryn Ross
DANGEROUS GAME	Margaret Mayo
SWEET BRIDE OF REVENGE	Suzanne Carey

Enchanted™

SHOTGUN BRIDEGROOM	Day Leclaire
FARELLI'S WIFE	Lucy Gordon
UNDERCOVER FIANCÉE	Rebecca Winters
MARRIED FOR A MONTH	Jessica Hart
HER OWN PRINCE CHARMING	Eva Rutland
BACHELOR COWBOY	Patricia Knoll
BIG BAD DAD	Christie Ridgway
WEDDING DAY BABY	Moyra Tarling

On sale from 2nd July 1999

H1 9906

Available at most branches of WH Smith, Tesco, Asda, Martins, Borders, Easons, Volume One/James Thin and most good paperback bookshops

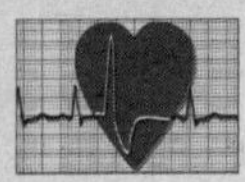  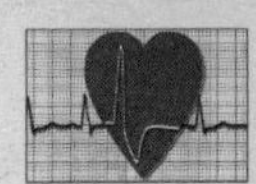

COMING NEXT MONTH

MORE THAN A MISTRESS by Alison Roberts

Anna's first House Officer job was in surgeon Michael Smith's hospital. She couldn't believe this was the same man she'd met on holiday, and parted from so badly. And Michael was no happier to see her!

A SURGEON FOR SUSAN by Helen Shelton

Susan was appalled when her sister set her up with a blind date! But Adam had been equally set up, by *his* sister. He was *so* gorgeous, why would anyone think he needed help finding a woman?

HOME AT LAST by Jennifer Taylor
A Country Practice—the third of four books.

After a year away Holly Ross felt able to come home. Many changes awaited her, not least a new stepmother. But the biggest change of all was her growing feelings for Dr Sam O'Neill, the partnership locum.

HEART-THROB by Meredith Webber
Bachelor Doctors

Peter's photo was plastered on *Hospital Heart-throb of the month* posters, embarrassing him when Anna came to work with him in A&E. She was intriguing and mysterious, and Peter couldn't help being fascinated. But he'd managed to stay a bachelor this far...

Available from 2nd July 1999

Available at most branches of WH Smith, Tesco, Asda, Martins, Borders, Easons, Volume One/James Thin and most good paperback bookshops

The perfect way to relax this summer!

Four stories from best selling
Mills & Boon® authors

Vicki Lewis Thompson

JoAnn Ross

Janice Kaiser

Stephanie Bond

*Enjoy the fun, the drama
and the excitement!*

On sale from 21st May 1999

*Available at most branches of WH Smith, Tesco, Asda,
Martins, Borders, Easons, Volume One / James Thin
and most good paperback bookshops*

We would like to take this opportunity to thank you for reading this Mills & Boon® book by offering you the chance to take FOUR more specially selected titles from the Enchanted™ series absolutely FREE! We're also making this offer to introduce you to the benefits of the Reader Service™—

- ★ FREE home delivery
- ★ FREE monthly Newsletter
- ★ FREE gifts and competitions
- ★ Exclusive Reader Service discounts
- ★ Books available before they're in the shops

Accepting these FREE books and gift places you under no obligation to buy; you may cancel at any time, even after receiving your free shipment. Simply complete your details below and return the entire page to the address below. **You don't even need a stamp!**

YES! Please send me 4 free Enchanted books and a surprise gift. I understand that unless you hear from me, I will receive 6 superb new titles every month for just £2.40 each, postage and packing free. I am under no obligation to purchase any books and may cancel my subscription at any time. The free books and gift will be mine to keep in any case.

N9EC

Ms/Mrs/Miss/Mr ....Initials..

BLOCK CAPITALS PLEASE

Surname..

Address..

....

....Postcode ....

Send this whole page to:
THE READER SERVICE, FREEPOST CN81, CROYDON, CR9 3WZ
(Eire readers please send coupon to: P.O. Box 4546, Dublin 24.)

Offer valid in UK and Eire only and not available to current Reader Service subscribers to this series. We reserve the right to refuse an application and applicants must be aged 18 years or over. Only one application per household. Terms and prices subject to change without notice. Offer expires 31st December 1999. As a result of this application, you may receive further offers from Harlequin Mills & Boon and other carefully selected companies. If you would prefer not to share in this opportunity please write to The Data Manager at the address above.

Mills & Boon is a registered trademark owned by Harlequin Mills & Boon Limited.
Enchanted is being used as a trademark.

Look out for the third volume in this limited collection of Regency Romances from Mills & Boon® in July.

Featuring:

Dear Lady Disdain
by Paula Marshall

and

An Angel's Touch
by Elizabeth Bailey

Still only £4.99

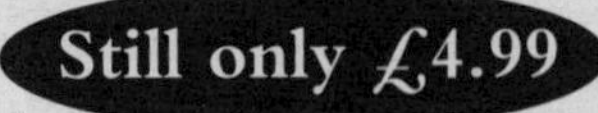

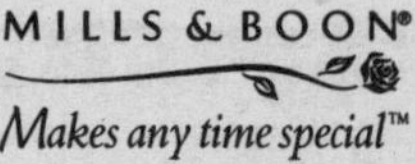

Available at most branches of WH Smith, Tesco, Martins, Borders, Easons, Volume One/James Thin and most good paperback bookshops